The Jungle

Also from EATMS Productions

Books on power, survival, women's autonomy, and the systems shaping modern America.

Nonfiction

Billionaires, Capitalism, and Power

Evil and the Mountain Ungreed
Self Help for American Billionaires
Selfish Steve and the Ivory Tower
Tariffs, Taxes, & Face-Eating Leopards
Ban Billionaires: Fascism Fix

Fascism, Religion, and Cultural Control

Self Help for the Manosphere
Fascism 2025
Fascism & the Perverts & the Greed Virus
Christian Fascism Marriage Book
Tyranny, Table Manners, & Tiramisu

Guides for Women's Autonomy and Protection

How to Survive in Post-America as a Woman
Project 2025 American Drag
4B – Burn, Ban, Boycott, Build
4B OG – So No Go GYN
I'm Glad He's Dead

Analysis of Authoritarian Project 2025

Project 2025: The Blueprint
Project 2025: The List
Project 2025, Christian Dumb Dumbs, & The Republican Agenda
Fascism, Project 2025, & The Pinkprint

Modern Rewrites for Women

Stoic Principles Reimagined
Siddhartha Reimagined
The Prince Reimagined for Women
The Art of War Reimagined for Women
The Jungle Reimagined
The Constitution Reimagined for Women

Machine Learning Series

AI, Bitcoin, Nostr for Women
AI, Safety, & Security for Women
AI, Anxiety, & Health for Women
AI, Kids, & Family Safety for Women
AI, Creativity, & Personal Expression for Women
AI, Independent Work, & Parallel Power for Women

Social Systems Series

Emotional Labor for Women
Household Power for Women
Workplace Power for Women
Medical Bias for Women
Aging Systems for Women
Recovery Systems for Women

Fiction

Dystopian Stories of Resistance and Collapse

Propaganda Paige & the Missing Prosperity
Propaganda Paige & the TIDE Manifesto
Propaganda Paige & the Shadow Cartographers
Propaganda Paige & the Prosperity Alliance
Propaganda Paige & the Shattered Truth
Propaganda Paige & the Rising TIDE
Propaganda Paige & the Last Bastion
Propaganda Paige & the Dawn of Prosperity
Project 2025: Dorian — The Last Men
Project 2025: Boy — A Last Men Novel

The Jungle Reimagined For 2025

Capitalism v. Humanity

by

Helena Hemmings

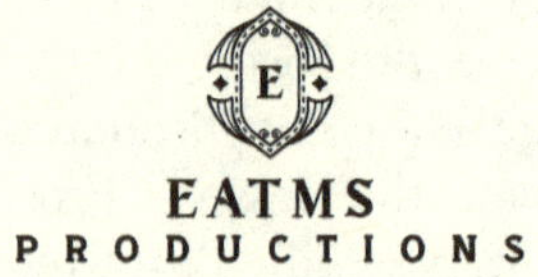

This title is part of an ongoing body of work. All EATMS Productions titles, across all series, authors, and formats, are components of a single connected project.

This book is a work of opinion and creative interpretation. While some names and events may be referenced or alluded to, any claims made are based on publicly available information and are intended as satire, parody, or commentary on societal and political issues. The content should not be interpreted as factual assertions about any individual or entity. The author does not intend to defraud, defame, or mislead, and encourages readers to form their own conclusions. Any resemblance to real persons, living or dead, is purely coincidental unless explicitly noted otherwise.

ISBN: 978-1-966014-18-8

Cover, interior design, interior prints by: Esme Mees

eatms@pm.me
www.eatms.me

Printed in the United States of America.

All that harms labor is treason to America.

— Abraham Lincoln

Table of Contents

Introduction
Welcome to the Oligarchy

Once upon a time, America prided itself on being a land of opportunity. A place where, if you worked hard enough, kept your head down, and put in the hours, you could build something for yourself, something lasting. It was a fairy tale told to immigrants as they stepped onto Ellis Island and to factory workers as they clocked into twelve-hour shifts. It was a story whispered through generations, passed down like a birthright, a promise of prosperity just waiting to be seized. And then, in 1906, a man named Upton Sinclair ripped the mask off that myth with a book called *The Jungle.* It was not a novel, not really. It was a cry of rage, an expose, a furious indictment of a capitalist system that ground human beings into dust for the sake of profit. He set his story in the slaughterhouses of Chicago, where men toiled in filth, where fingers and limbs disappeared into machinery, where bodies were chewed up just as surely as the cattle hanging from rusted hooks. And America gasped, not at the suffering of the workers, but at the revelation that their food might be tainted. The outrage that followed led to the Meat Inspection Act and the Pure Food and Drug Act of 1906, laws meant to reassure the public that their sausages were free of rat poison and tuberculosis-ridden beef. The suffering of the laborers? Well, that was simply an unfortunate side effect of industry.

Sinclair famously lamented that he had aimed for the heart but hit the stomach. But in doing so, he accidentally proved his own thesis: in a system ruled by profit, human beings were incidental, collateral damage at best, inconveniences at worst. It was not the plight of the worker that stirred Washington to act; it was the dawning horror that American consumers might get sick. And so, while the food got cleaner, the workers remained in their squalor, shackled to an economic system that saw them as disposable parts in the great machine of progress. Capitalism, after all, has always been far more invested in protecting its product than its people. The early 20th century was an era of robber barons and monopolists, industrial titans who owned entire industries and bent government to their will. Men like Rockefeller and Carnegie constructed their empires on the backs of underpaid laborers, and when those workers dared to demand fair wages or safer conditions, they were met with Pinkerton thugs, club-wielding police, and mass layoffs. The government did not protect the worker; it protected the company.

But labor fought back. Unionization surged, strikes swept across the country, and the working class clawed out hard-fought protections, minimum wages, the forty-hour workweek, child labor laws. By the mid-century, there was at least the illusion of balance, a sense that capitalism and democracy could coexist without one wholly consuming the other. But illusions do not last. What Sinclair revealed in *The Jungle* was not just a failure of regulation, nor was it merely an exposé of meatpacking horrors. He had peeled back the layers of an economic system whose primary function was, and remains, to extract as much profit from human lives as possible before discarding them. A hundred years later, that system has evolved. The slaughterhouses of 1906 have been replaced by the warehouse gulags of Amazon, the digital sweatshops of Uber, the faceless, omnipresent surveillance of gig work. The tools have changed. The cruelty remains.

We no longer send children into coal mines, but we do force families to work multiple jobs, to deliver groceries and drive strangers for a few dollars a ride, all while an algorithm determines their worth in fractions of a cent. We no longer have factories with floors slick with blood and grease; instead, we have fulfillment centers where workers collapse from exhaustion, where bathroom breaks are tracked, where bodies are scanned like inventory. And we still have billionaires who believe they are entitled to it all. Jeff Bezos, Elon Musk, the tech lords of Silicon Valley, these are our Carnegies and Rockefellers, our modern-day monopolists who own not just industries but the very platforms that dictate reality. They do not simply own the means of production; they own the means of communication, the infrastructure of thought itself. And yet, they insist that they are innovators, pioneers, visionaries of a grand new world.

Welcome to the Oligarchy. We are living in the twilight of democracy, watching as capitalism sheds even the pretense of fairness and reveals itself in its final form: techno-feudalism. The future that Sinclair warned of has arrived, but it has been streamlined, digitized, and automated. Today, workers do not have a boss they can see or a factory floor they can walk away from. Their overseer is an algorithm, an invisible god that determines whether they eat or starve, that adjusts their wages in real-time, that punishes them for slowing down. There are no unions in this new jungle. There are no strikes against an app. How do you picket against an invisible hand? The worker of 2025 is not a man with a lunch pail walking into a factory; she is a woman juggling four gig jobs, a driver-for-hire who sleeps in her car, a grocery deliverer who waits in a parking lot for an order that might never come. She is the invisible labor force, scattered and isolated, each worker an island kept just desperate enough to avoid rebellion.

And yet, rebellion will come. Because the lie of the American Dream is cracking once again, and people are beginning to see the truth. Sinclair's jungle was made of steel and blood; ours is made of data and code, but the outcome is the same: profit extracted from suffering, billionaires fattening themselves on the broken backs of the working class. And history tells us that no system, no matter how entrenched, lasts forever. The future belongs to those who dare to seize it. And if we have learned anything from the past century, it is that the time to fight back is always now.

It is easy to imagine that we have evolved past the horrors Upton Sinclair exposed in *The Jungle*. After all, the meatpacking plants of the early 1900s were filthy, unregulated death traps. They were places where limbs were lost, where disease spread unchecked, where men were broken by the brutal, unrelenting grind of industrial capitalism. The laws passed in response to Sinclair's work, though limited, did make a difference. They sanitized the process. They forced the hand of regulation, if only to protect consumers. And for a while, there was a sense that progress had been made, that we had left those dark days behind. But capitalism does not learn lessons; it merely adapts. It is not deterred by outrage; it is refined by it. The same system that once let men fall into rendering vats and be ground into lard has not disappeared; it has simply become more efficient. It has moved from factories to platforms, from assembly lines to cloud servers. It has found new ways to extract labor, to strip workers of protections, to turn human beings into disposable assets.

This is the world of 2025, where a billion-dollar empire can be run from a smartphone, where workers never set foot in an office, where employment is a transactional arrangement with no benefits, no guarantees, no stability. The modern worker is no longer a cog in a machine, they are the machine itself, expected to optimize their output, to be constantly available, to function with the precision of an algorithm while remaining utterly replaceable. They are rated, tracked, and assessed by unseen forces. Their wages shift based on demand, calculated in real time by profit-maximizing formulas that strip away human need in favor of corporate gain. It is not that conditions have improved; it is that capitalism has found a way to eliminate the evidence of suffering. No bloodstained floors, no public outcry, just a quiet, systematic extraction of human effort through a screen.

Take the modern warehouse, for example, the fulfillment centers of corporations like Amazon, which operate with a level of dehumanization Sinclair could not have imagined. Workers are monitored down to the second, their movements scrutinized, their pace dictated by AI-driven quotas that push their bodies past the point of exhaustion. Injury rates soar. And yet, because the floor is not visibly slick with gore, because there is no immediate spectacle of brutality, the outrage is muted. The cruelty of the modern workplace is not in its chaos but in its precision. The factory floor has become an algorithm. The assembly line is now an app. And the worker, always replaceable, always one misstep away from termination, is trapped in an invisible cage.

Then there is the gig economy, the great capitalist sleight of hand that convinces workers they are free, that they are their own bosses, that they have autonomy when, in reality, they are at the mercy of systems even more ruthless than those of the industrial era. The gig worker does not have a contract. They do not have a pension. They do not have health care, paid time off, or workplace protections. They have an app, an algorithm, and the ever-present threat of deactivation. A low rating can mean financial ruin. An arbitrary policy change can erase their income overnight. They are not employees, because to be an employee is to have rights, to have some form of leverage. Instead, they are contractors, independent in name only, bound to the whims of faceless corporations that take no responsibility for their well-being. They work for platforms that claim to offer opportunity but, in reality, offer nothing more than subsistence. They are the new working class: fragmented, precarious, and expendable.

And as this new jungle takes shape, as the modern labor force is reshaped into something more diffuse, more isolated, more vulnerable, the old questions remain. Who benefits from this system? Who profits from this so-called innovation? The answer is the same as it was in Sinclair's time: the oligarchs, the corporate overlords, the men who own the means of production, except now, the production is data, logistics, and digital labor. Jeff Bezos, Elon Musk, Mark Zuckerberg, and their ilk do not need factories. They do not need smokestacks. They own the infrastructure of modern life itself. They own the platforms that dictate who is seen, who is heard, who gets paid, and who disappears. They have built an empire that stretches across the digital landscape, one that shapes economies, elections, and public discourse. And they have done it while convincing the public that this is progress.

But progress for whom? The billionaire class has perfected the art of presenting exploitation as opportunity, of branding wage slavery as flexibility, of making the working class believe that they are just one investment, one startup, one hustle away from breaking free. They have repackaged the old dream, the idea that through sheer determination, anyone can rise to the top. But the top is already owned. The gates are locked. The wealth hoarded. The reality of 2025 is not that capitalism has become kinder, but that it has become smarter. It does not need armed guards to break strikes when it can prevent organizing entirely. It does not need to outlaw unions when it can replace every striking worker with an automated system. It does not need to silence dissent when it can simply drown it in the algorithmic noise of infinite content.

This is the dawning of a new economic order, not one of freedom but of feudalism, where the tech elite hold the power once wielded by kings, where the working class is reduced to digital serfs, forever chasing an algorithm they can never beat. And the question remains: how long before the workers of this new jungle recognize their chains? How long before they realize that they are not free? That their so-called independence is a carefully curated illusion, designed to keep them complacent, to keep them hungry, to keep them moving just fast enough to survive but never fast enough to escape? The Jungle of 1906 was brutal, but it was visible. The Jungle of 2025 is far more insidious. It is wrapped in the language of efficiency, innovation, and progress, but beneath that glossy exterior, the same truth remains: the worker is nothing more than a resource to be extracted, used up, and discarded.

Upton Sinclair's greatest tragedy was that his warnings went unheeded. His novel led to regulatory changes, yes, but the system endured. It adapted. It found new ways to exploit, to dehumanize, to profit off the backs of the many for the benefit of the few. And now, more than a century later, we find ourselves at the edge of another precipice, watching as capitalism once again reinvents itself, as it refines its methods, as it tightens its grip. The question is no longer whether we recognize the injustice, because we do. It is will we fight back.

The defining characteristic of every oligarchy, every system of control that has ever existed, is its ability to convince the people beneath it that there is no alternative. That this is simply the way things are, that history has ended, that to fight back is to fight against the natural order itself. The feudal lords of the Middle Ages insisted that the hierarchy of peasants, vassals, and kings was divine will, that to resist was to defy not just law but

God himself. The industrial titans of Sinclair's era justified their stranglehold on labor by claiming that competition was the ultimate truth, that if a man could not survive in the market, then he did not deserve to. And today, the tech billionaires who rule our modern jungle weave the same narrative with updated terminology, with data-driven rhetoric, with the cold, mechanical language of efficiency. They tell us that the gig economy is about freedom, that automation is about progress, that the collapse of stable employment is simply the price of innovation. They do not need to force compliance through violence; they manufacture it through exhaustion, through distraction, through the slow, creeping erosion of hope.

Because that is the real trick, the final, perfected mechanism of control: not just the destruction of unions or the suppression of organizing, but the removal of the very belief that change is possible. When workers are no longer bound together in factories, when their struggles are isolated, individualized, reduced to personal failures rather than systemic ones, the possibility of revolution dims. Who do you strike against when your employer is an algorithm? Where do you protest when your boss is an app? How do you resist when the system convinces you that there is no system at all, just a marketplace of opportunities, just an endless race for survival in which some will make it and some will not?

This is the great myth of the 21st century: that we are all free agents, that we are all just one hustle away from security, that if we suffer, if we struggle, if we cannot afford rent or medical care or even a day off, it is because we have not worked hard enough. Not because the game is rigged. Not because the wealth of the world is hoarded in tax havens, siphoned into stock buybacks, locked away by a handful of men who have convinced themselves that they deserve it. The billionaires of today do not see themselves as exploiters; they see themselves as visionaries. They build rockets while their workers sleep in their cars. They host TED Talks on philanthropy while union organizers are fired in retaliation. They brand themselves as geniuses, as innovators, as the architects of a future that, conveniently, will never arrive for the people who labor to build it.

But here's the thing about history: it does not end. No system is permanent. No empire lasts forever. And the cracks are already beginning to show. The workers of the modern jungle are not as powerless as the oligarchs would have them believe. The tech-driven economy has not erased the need for human labor; it has only disguised it, hidden it beneath layers of software and digital abstraction. But the reality remains: packages still need to be shipped, food still needs to be delivered, data still needs to be processed, products still need to be made. The power of labor is not gone, it has simply been scattered, fragmented, forced into isolation. But isolation is not an inevitability. The same technology that allows corporations to extract labor with surgical precision also allows workers to organize in ways never before possible. The internet, for all its flaws, remains a tool of connection, of communication, of opposition.

Already, we are seeing the first waves of defiance: strikes at Amazon warehouses, walkouts by gig workers demanding fair pay, digital platforms where workers share information, exposing the lies of corporate PR. The jungle is not silent. It is restless. And history has shown us, again and again, that when workers begin to recognize their power, when they begin to see through the illusion, when they understand that they are not isolated but part of something larger, change is inevitable. The great lie of capitalism has always been that the worker is replaceable. But when workers move together, when they act as a force rather than as individuals, they are not replaceable, they are unstoppable.

This is the moment we find ourselves in, the threshold between despair and rebellion, between complacency and action. The choice before us is the same choice that faced the workers of Sinclair's time: accept the conditions handed down from above, or refuse them. Accept the scraps thrown by billionaires, or demand the wealth we create. Accept the future they have planned for us, or build one of our own.

And that is the final truth, the one that no algorithm, no billionaire, no digital overlord can erase: the future belongs to those who claim it. The Jungle of 1906 led to reforms, to regulations, to temporary victories in the fight for labor rights.

But the jungle was never cleared away, it was only rearranged, rebranded, given a sleek user interface and a PR-friendly facade. Today, in 2025, we face the same battle in a new form. The question is not whether the jungle exists. The question is whether we will let it stand.

1
The New Frontier

The city stretched before them like a great, glimmering behemoth, its skyline pulsing with neon promises and holographic assurances of prosperity. Joras had imagined this moment a thousand times, his family stepping off the mag-lev transport, their meager belongings packed tightly into a single bag, the scent of possibility thick in the air. It was the promise of the new world, the grand myth of opportunity that had drawn millions before him, each one convinced that this city, this system, would be different. The buildings were taller, the technology more advanced, but the dream remained the same. Here, in the capital of the algorithmic empire, the marketplace of the future, he would find work. He would carve out a place for his wife, Ona, and their young son, Miklas. He would prove that they had not traveled across continents, through checkpoints and border scans and biometric gates, just to fail.

The station's doors hissed open, releasing them into a surge of people moving in orchestrated urgency, their movements dictated by the silent pulses of their wrist implants, guiding them to the next task, the next ride, the next transaction. Joras hesitated only a moment before gripping Ona's hand and pulling her forward. She squeezed back, her grip firm, her face unreadable. She had been the skeptical one. She had questioned the plan, questioned the reality beneath the advertisements, questioned whether a life built on gig contracts and data scoring could ever be anything more than digital serfdom. But Joras had convinced her. Had told her that they were different, that they were willing to work harder, longer, faster than those who had failed before them. That this city, this glittering metropolis of infinite connectivity and boundless efficiency, would reward their determination.

They emerged onto the street, blinking against the cascade of light from the towers above. Capitalschism billboards flared across the skyline, their slogans shifting with every passerby. *Work smarter, live freer. Optimize your future. Your potential is limitless.* The words wrapped around them like a digital cocoon, weaving a narrative of opportunity so compelling, so omnipresent, that for a moment Joras let himself believe it. He had spent months studying the job markets, the employment rankings, the pathways to success in this city of endless transactions. He had watched the success stories, the testimonials of those who had arrived with nothing and ascended to wealth in a matter of years. He had read the manuals, the guides on how to maximize one's algorithmic score, how to ensure constant employment, how to outmaneuver the countless others scrambling for a foothold. He had told himself that he would not fall behind, that he would master the system before it could master him.

But as they walked through the district, reality began to creep in at the edges of the illusion. The streets were clean, the air purified, the pathways lined with glowing strips that guided foot traffic in optimized patterns, but the faces around them were tight with the unmistakable strain of people living on borrowed time. Men and women in identical slate-gray workwear moved with machine-like precision, their eyes scanning notifications projected into the air in front of them, their expressions carefully neutral. The ones who stopped, who hesitated, who fumbled with their devices, were met with impatient sidesteps, with dismissive glances, with the quiet, suffocating pressure of a system that demanded constant motion. And then there were the others, the ones who lingered at the edges of the sidewalks, watching the flow of efficiency from just beyond its borders. They wore no workwear. Their hands held no devices. They did not move with purpose. They were still. And in this city, stillness was the first sign of failure.

Ona felt it before he did. She slowed her pace, taking in the storefronts that flashed promotional offers tailored to their profiles. Rental pods available with flexible payment plans. Dietary subscriptions designed for peak cognitive function. Employment packages promising optimal earning potential. Everything designed to guide them toward seamless integration, toward participation, toward productivity. But she saw the gaps. The cracks where the façade faltered. The small, near-invisible alcoves where people sat curled against the walls, their devices dark, their clothing worn thin at the seams. The alleyways where delivery drones hovered, scanning the barcodes of discarded belongings before whisking them away. The way the city absorbed and erased its inefficiencies with quiet, clinical precision.

Joras pushed forward, unwilling to let doubt settle in. They had a plan. He had studied the market, had arranged their first contract before they had even arrived. He pulled up his interface, his credentials syncing to the city's network. His score was neutral, neither promising nor damning. It was a start. He turned to Ona, offering her the reassurance he knew she needed. "We're here," he said, forcing conviction into his voice. "We made it."

She looked at him for a long moment before nodding. "Let's hope that means something."

The first cracks in the illusion came quickly. The moment Joras activated his work profile, the city's endless, ambient hum of efficiency took on a new, more menacing rhythm. His interface pulsed with incoming bids, job offers flashing and vanishing in seconds, each one requiring an instant decision. The numbers flickered too fast to absorb, each task measured in minutes, each payment adjusted in real-time based on demand. It was a game, one he had spent months preparing for, but the reality of it felt different. The sense of control he had imagined was an illusion, there was no choosing, no negotiation. There was only speed. He hesitated for a fraction too long on his first offer, a warehouse shift with a high-demand surge bonus, and the slot vanished, claimed by someone quicker, someone more desperate. He gritted his teeth and waited for another. It came, a delivery route across the sector, a five-hour block. He accepted, and just like that, he was absorbed into the machine.

The city wasted no time integrating him. His path illuminated, his navigation recalibrated, his every step tracked and optimized for peak efficiency. A rental e-bike unlocked at his approach, its cost deducted in real-time from his first payment. There was no money exchanged, no contracts signed. The system moved faster than thought, weaving every action into a seamless transaction. Joras rode through the streaming lanes, past towers wrapped in glowing advertisements, past storefronts where robotic clerks filled orders with mechanized precision, past streets that pulsed with a constant, orchestrated flow. It was mesmerizing. It was terrifying. It was exactly what he had signed up for.

But then, just beneath the surface, came the realization that this system, so smooth, so frictionless, demanded absolute submission. His first stop was a corporate apartment tower, its facade pristine, its entrance scanning his credentials before allowing him inside. The delivery was contactless; he placed the package in the drop slot, waited for confirmation, and was instantly assigned his next task. No human interaction. No acknowledgment. Just a score adjustment, a recalibration of his standing in the system, an invisible metric determining whether he would be offered better jobs or relegated to the bottom of the algorithm's hierarchy. Every movement carried weight, every pause a potential penalty. He kept going.

Ona had set up her own profile that morning, her credentials syncing seamlessly, her opportunities funneling in just as fast as his. But her experience was different. As a new applicant with no work history in the system, her offers were scarce, the pay rates lower, the penalties harsher. Her first task came after nearly an hour of waiting: a data-tagging job, remote, low-paid, and requiring an instant response time to avoid wage penalties. She accepted, and the system swallowed her whole. There was no onboarding, no instruction. A list of digital images appeared before her, each one requiring classification, objects, faces, locations. The interface measured her speed, her accuracy, her efficiency. If she slowed, the task pool adjusted, deprioritizing her. If she made a mistake, the system logged it, affecting her ranking. It was work without a workplace, labor without acknowledgment, a job she could lose without ever speaking to a human being.

By midday, the pressure was palpable. Joras and Ona checked their earnings, their status, their algorithmic placement. Their combined income was lower than expected, the hidden fees and deductions more aggressive than advertised. The cost of renting a mobility device, the automated maintenance fees, the insurance surcharges, all quietly subtracted from their balance. The city had no need for outright theft; it simply rewrote the terms of survival in ways that ensured no one ever truly got ahead. Even success, Joras realized, was a kind of failure, because it meant deeper entrenchment, a tighter bond to the system, an existence that could be erased with a single algorithmic adjustment.

Miklas, too young to understand the weight settling onto his parents, played with the city's public interfaces, tracing glowing patterns on interactive walls, laughing at the holographic birds that flitted between the towers. For him, the city was still a place of wonder. Joras envied him. He watched as his son reached for the projections, trying to touch something that wasn't real. The metaphor was too obvious, too painful. He looked away.

They met that evening in their rental pod, a small, windowless unit that was neither home nor shelter but a temporary concession from the city, a holding place for those still proving themselves worthy of permanence. The walls adjusted their color temperature, the air filtered to perfection, the interface listing their daily performance metrics with clinical detachment. Joras sat beside Ona, their bodies pressed into the too-small seating area, their exhaustion mirrored in each other's faces. Miklas slept between them, his small body curled into itself, his breathing steady, unaware of the calculations surrounding him, his parents' work scores, their income projections, their rapidly depleting balance. The city did not wait for children to grow. The moment he reached a certain age, the system would decide his trajectory, measuring his potential like it measured everything else. It had already begun, in small ways, offering pre-selected educational modules, assigning aptitude scores, feeding data into the network that would determine his place long before he had a chance to choose it himself.

"Did you eat?" Ona asked softly.

He hadn't. He didn't want to see the deduction reflected in his balance. Every meal had a cost, every break a consequence. He exhaled, resting his head back against the cool, synthetic wall. "Tomorrow will be better."

Ona didn't argue. But she didn't agree, either.

The second day began before the first had properly ended. The city never stopped, never paused, never allowed a moment of stillness without consequence. Joras woke to a notification pulse, his contract queue had updated overnight, new offers flooding in as the system recalculated demand. The highest-paying shift started in fifteen minutes. He had to be out the door in five. His body screamed for rest, but rest was not an option. He slipped out of bed without waking Miklas, glanced at Ona, who was already awake, already checking her own queue, and nodded. There was no discussion. No strategy session. They both understood now. This was not about finding opportunity. It was about keeping up.

Joras moved through the streets as one among thousands, indistinguishable from the rest of the city's invisible workforce, each person moving along their assigned path like a piece in a vast, unknowable machine. He felt the weight of it now, the constant, suffocating expectation of speed, precision, optimization. The system learned him as he worked, adjusted its demands accordingly. When he moved too slowly between deliveries, his route efficiency rating ticked downward, imperceptible at first, then suddenly, critically low. A red warning flashed. *Suboptimal performance detected. Future job availability impacted.* He pushed harder, rode faster, ignored the burn in his legs as he navigated the city's arterial lanes, dodging other workers, drones, automated transports. The skyline, the glass and steel promise of something greater, blurred past him. He no longer looked up.

Ona's work was no less ruthless. She had cycled through six different microtasks before noon, each one discarded when her speed failed to meet the algorithm's shifting expectations. The facial recognition database she had been tagging was suddenly at capacity, contract revoked, earnings forfeited. The translation gig required a fluency rating she had no way of proving, rejected. The market research survey paid pennies per completion but tracked time spent answering, too fast, disqualified; too slow, disqualified. She watched her earnings fluctuate, tick upward in fragments, trickle away in hidden deductions. By midday, the sum total of her labor was barely enough to cover the rental fee for their pod. She did not stop working.

Joras' exhaustion turned to numbness, then something worse, a creeping understanding that survival in this city was not about intelligence or skill or even endurance. It was about compliance. About adapting, faster and faster, to the shifting, unpredictable conditions of a system that never stopped learning, never stopped refining its methods of extraction. The city was not a place. It was a process. A machine designed not to house people, but to use them.

And not everyone made it.

That afternoon, Joras saw his first collapse. A worker, not much older than him, crumpled in the intersection of two transit lanes, his body folding inward as if trying to disappear. He had been running a route, Joras recognized the delivery harness, the same company-issued pack weighing down his own shoulders, but now, his device had locked him out. A low-efficiency rating? A missed shift? An expired work permit? It didn't matter. He no longer belonged to the city's workforce, and without that, he no longer existed.

Joras slowed, barely registering the irritated pings of those forced to navigate around the obstruction. The fallen worker's eyes were open, staring through the neon haze of the skyline, unfocused. His hands twitched slightly at his sides, like he was trying to reenter the system, trying to reconnect to something that had already discarded him. A drone hovered overhead, scanning, logging the incident. Joras knew how this ended. There were no ambulances, no rescue crews. The city did not rescue. It cleaned. The worker would be gone in minutes, erased from the street, his belongings cataloged and redistributed, his absence noted only as a statistical adjustment in the efficiency database.

A hand gripped Joras' arm, pulling him forward. Ona. She had found him, had seen the scene, had known, instinctively, that he was hesitating. That he was about to make the mistake of caring. Her grip tightened.

"Don't," she whispered.

He followed her without protest.
That evening, as they lay in their rental pod, Miklas curled between them, the walls flashing ambient light to induce optimal sleep efficiency, Joras whispered, "How long do you think we have?"

Ona didn't answer. Didn't need to. He already knew.

Outside, the city continued its seamless operation, oblivious to the lives within it. Joras had once thought of it as something greater than himself, a vast and unknowable force, something powerful and permanent. But now he saw it for what it was, a machine, built to extract, to optimize, to discard. It was not malevolent, not intentionally cruel. It simply functioned as designed. But that was the true horror, wasn't it? That it did not need to be cruel. It only needed to be efficient.

Ona shifted beside him, exhaling softly. Her fingers brushed against his wrist, against the faint glow of his work tracker. He could see her own beneath her sleeve, the same sterile, quiet presence that dictated their days, their survival. They were measured, assessed, assigned. They would work until the system no longer required them. And then, like the worker Joras had seen on the street, they would be erased.

But not yet. Not tomorrow.

Joras let his eyes close, let his body settle into the rhythm of artificial sleep, the walls dimming into the regulated cycle the city had set for them. The machine would wake him when it needed him. He had learned that much.

Somewhere, deep in the layers of data that ran the city, their scores were being adjusted, their assignments refined, their usefulness recalculated. The system was preparing for another day, another cycle, another round of labor to be extracted.

And they, like all the others, would comply.

2
The Factory of the 21st Century

The onboarding process took less than thirty seconds. There was no handshake, no welcome speech, no human interaction at all, just the sterile glow of a biometric scanner and a notification confirming his employment status. A chime sounded, followed by a message projected onto the screen in front of him: *Welcome, Associate. Your credentials have been verified. You are now optimized for workflow integration.* Below it, his shift details auto-generated in real time, adjusting to company demand. His first assignment would begin in exactly six minutes.

Joras blinked, staring at the message as if it might change, as if something more substantial might follow. But nothing did. The machine had made its decision, and that was that. He had expected something else, maybe an orientation, a manager explaining the finer details, some indication that he was stepping into a workplace rather than being absorbed into an unseen mechanism. Instead, it was only the quiet, seamless judgment of an algorithm that had calculated his value and slotted him accordingly.

The facility doors slid open, and he stepped forward, drawn into the great, humming body of Capitalschism.

He had seen images before, on public feeds, in company-sponsored documentaries that painted it as the pinnacle of modern logistics, an architectural marvel of precision and efficiency. But the reality of it was something else entirely. The scale was almost incomprehensible. The ceiling stretched high above, embedded with long, glowing strips of artificial daylight that never dimmed, never flickered, never changed. It was a sky that never knew time. Beneath it, a vast, sprawling landscape of automated conveyor systems and towering sorting stations extended in all directions, an engineered labyrinth where movement never ceased. Robots glided along designated pathways, robotic arms pivoted and extended with inhuman speed, machines hummed and whirred in constant, ceaseless rhythm. There was no wasted motion, no hesitation, no disorder. Everything operated in perfect harmony.

And then there were the workers. They were human, but only barely visible within the machinery, their presence an afterthought, a necessary inefficiency. They moved in synchronized lines, dressed in identical gray uniforms without insignias, their bodies directed entirely by the interfaces on their wrists. No conversations. No casual movements. Just labor, precise and uninterrupted, dictated by algorithms that knew their capabilities better than they did. Joras had never seen anything like it. He had spent years working in labor-heavy environments, but this was something different. This was not a workplace. It was a process. A closed-loop system designed not to employ people, but to extract from them, to push them toward maximum efficiency until they either adapted or failed.

His wrist buzzed. *Proceed to Station 11-G.*

A thin blue line appeared on the floor, projected by an unseen source, illuminating the most optimized path for him to follow. It curved and adjusted as he moved, ensuring he would arrive at his station with no wasted steps, no deviations. He obeyed, stepping into the flow of workers, matching their pace, his body already falling into sync with the factory's rhythm.

The deeper he moved into the facility, the more oppressive the silence became. The sheer scale of the place should have been deafening, so many bodies, so much motion, but there was no natural sound, no voices, no human interruptions. The machines worked without complaint. The workers had learned to do the same.

He arrived at his station. A standing desk, a glowing interface, a conveyor system that fed packages into his workspace at timed intervals. Above him, a floating display projected his metrics, efficiency, accuracy, speed. Each was set at baseline, a neutral position that would shift depending on his performance. A soft chime rang in his ear, followed by the automated voice of the system: *Task Initiation Confirmed. Welcome to the Workflow.*

The first package slid into place. A barcode appeared on the screen, flashing with a set of instructions. Joras scanned it, placed the package into its designated bin, and confirmed completion. The moment he did, the next package arrived. Then another. Then another.

The pace was relentless. There was no adjustment period, no gradual buildup. He was expected to match the rhythm immediately, to integrate seamlessly into the existing flow. If he hesitated, even for a second, a yellow notification pulsed at the edge of his vision: *Workflow Efficiency Warning.* If he moved too quickly, the system compensated, recalibrating his workload to ensure a steady, optimized output. The goal was not to complete a set amount of work. The goal was balance, his movements synchronized perfectly with the factory's demands, his speed dictated by an algorithm that allowed no room for variation.

Time lost meaning. There were no clocks, no shifts of light, no natural markers to signal the passing of hours. His body was the only thing that registered time, the slow burn in his muscles, the stiffness in his joints, the creeping sensation that he was being hollowed out by repetition. The only interruptions came when the system forced them.
A notification appeared: *Mandatory Rest Break Initiated. Five minutes.*

Five minutes. Not a second more, not a second less. The fatigue management software had detected a decrease in his efficiency, a minor but measurable decline, and had calculated the minimum necessary break period required to restore function. He stepped away from his station, following another glowing line toward the designated break area, a small, enclosed space with no chairs, no windows, only a hydration station and a biometric scanner that monitored vital signs. Other workers stood silently, leaning against the walls, eyes unfocused. No one spoke. The system had trained them well.

He took a drink from the hydration station, barely registering the taste, and exhaled. Five minutes. That was all he was allowed. Anything longer was inefficient. Anything shorter would impact overall productivity. He checked his performance metrics on his wrist. No penalties. Not yet.

His wrist buzzed. *Break Over. Resume Task.*

Joras returned to his station. The workflow resumed. He obeyed.

By the time his shift ended, he had processed thousands of packages. He had no memory of any single one. They had passed through his hands like streams of data, meaningless and indistinct, their destinations unknown, their contents irrelevant. He had moved mechanically, his body an extension of the factory, his mind reduced to simple inputs and outputs. He had thought he understood work. He had thought he had prepared for this. He had been wrong.

His exit path illuminated before him, guiding him toward the transit bay where workers were funneled out of the facility in waves. They moved in the same synchronized patterns, their shifts completed, their bodies emptied into the city like recycled waste.

His wrist buzzed again. *Shift Completed. Performance Logged. Review Pending.*

The system had judged him. Tomorrow, it would decide if he was worth keeping.

Outside, the city pulsed with neon light, a stark contrast to the cold sterility of the factory. He inhaled, expecting relief, but there was none. The work was done, but the machine had left its mark. He still felt the rhythm of it, the pull of the interface, the lingering sensation that his body was still moving through the workflow even as he stood still. The factory had released him, but only for now. He had been processed, optimized, integrated. Tomorrow, the system would call him back.

And somewhere, deep within the glowing towers of Capitalschism, the algorithm adjusted. It had learned from him. It had refined its expectations. It had recalibrated the workload.

Tomorrow, it would push harder.

And so would he.

Joras had expected exhaustion, but this was something else entirely. It was not the kind of tiredness that settled into his muscles, the kind that could be shaken off with a good meal or a long sleep. No, this exhaustion was something deeper, something woven into the fabric of his mind, a slow erosion of thought itself. When he closed his eyes, he saw the interface flashing numbers, his body instinctively reacting to commands that were no longer there. When he lay still, he felt the phantom hum of the conveyor beneath his fingertips, the weight of a thousand indistinguishable packages passing through his hands. The system had seeped into him, left its imprint in ways he could not define.

He moved through the next day in the same prescribed rhythm, his body obeying instructions before his mind could process them. The transition from sleep to work was seamless, dictated by the notification that pulsed through his wrist the moment his rest cycle ended. The algorithm had recalculated. His new shift assignment was not at the same station. That was the first lesson he had learned about Capitalschism, there was no routine, no comfort of familiarity. The company did not see workers as individuals with learned skills; it saw them as adaptable inputs, movable parts of a larger system, able to be reassigned and repurposed as needed. Yesterday, he had been a sorter. Today, he was a picker. Tomorrow, he might be something else entirely.

The path before him lit up once more, guiding him to his new station. The factory was too large, too labyrinthine to navigate on one's own. It was designed that way, to strip workers of autonomy, to ensure they relied entirely on the system to function. Joras followed the glowing line across the vast warehouse floor, past the silent rows of identical workers, past the robotic arms that never tired, never faltered, never needed recalibration. The factory did not acknowledge his presence. It did not acknowledge anyone's presence. It simply absorbed them.

His new task was simple in theory. Retrieve items from the automated storage units, confirm their barcodes, place them onto a designated conveyor. The complexity came in the pacing, in the brutal demand of speed, in the way the system tracked not just his movements but the milliseconds between them. A second too slow and his efficiency rating would drop. Two seconds too slow and the algorithm would flag him for review. Five seconds too slow and he would be marked as an underperformer, placing his entire employment in jeopardy.

There was no time to process what he was picking, no moment to reflect on the absurdity of it. He could have been retrieving anything, electronics, clothing, food, medical supplies. It did not matter. The only thing that mattered was speed. His hands became extensions of the scanner, his body a mere vehicle for transferring objects from one place to another. There was no artistry, no craftsmanship, no trace of humanity in the work. It was efficiency, stripped to its rawest, most merciless form.

Hours blurred together, marked only by the silent adjustments of the system, the way it recalibrated itself to his movements, always demanding just a little more, just a fraction of a second faster. It was never enough. It would never be enough. He understood that now. The moment he adapted, the moment he reached what should have been his limit, the system would shift the threshold. There was no endpoint, no plateau where the work became manageable. There was only acceleration, an infinite tightening of expectations, a race that could never be won.

The break notification came as both a relief and an insult. Five minutes. The system had determined that was the exact amount of time necessary to prevent him from collapsing. No more, no less. He stepped away from his station, following the designated path to the break area, where other workers stood in weary silence, their faces reflecting the same quiet realization. None of them spoke. There was nothing to say. They had all been absorbed into the same relentless process.

He took a sip of water from the hydration station, his mind still running through the motions of his task, his fingers twitching as if they were still grasping for phantom items. Five minutes. It was not enough to think, only enough to reset. To ensure that he could return to the line without resistance.

The break ended, and the machine reclaimed him.

Joras worked without questioning, without allowing himself the luxury of doubt. He had come here with the expectation of labor, but he had not understood the nature of this kind of work, the way it stripped a person down into something more, no, something less, than human. He had been prepared for exhaustion, for difficulty, for long shifts and sore muscles. He had not been prepared for this slow, methodical hollowing.

At some point, in the endless stretch of work, he made a mistake. It was small, barely a deviation, a misplaced item, a barcode scanned twice instead of once. A simple error, one that should have been insignificant. But the system registered it immediately. A red warning flashed across his interface. *Error detected. Productivity rating adjusted.*

His heart pounded. The warning stayed on the display, pulsing like an open wound, refusing to disappear. His breath came faster. He corrected the mistake, but the damage had been done. The rating did not return to its previous state. A single error, a single hesitation, had left a mark, an invisible scar in the system's perception of him. The algorithm would remember. It would recalculate his efficiency, factor his mistake into future assignments, adjust his workload accordingly.

There was no forgiveness in this place. No allowances for human error. The machine learned, adapted, optimized.

His shift ended, but the warning followed him. It stayed in his mind as he exited the factory, as he merged with the crowd of workers dispersing into the city, as he checked his performance log again and again, hoping the number had changed. It had not.

Outside, the night air should have been cool, but he did not feel it. The neon glow of the city washed over him, artificial and unwavering, the reflection of something vast and indifferent. He turned toward the transit hub, toward the temporary home that was never truly home, and realized with quiet horror that he was not leaving the factory at all.

The walls were gone, but the machine still held him. It had measured him, recorded him, placed him within its endless calculations. His mistake was logged, his efficiency rating adjusted. Tomorrow, the algorithm would decide how hard to push him, how much more it could extract before his body broke or his usefulness ran out.

Joras exhaled. He did not remember breathing at all that day.

Somewhere deep within Capitalschism, the machine recalibrated, adjusting for the new data. It had learned from him. Tomorrow, it would refine its methods. Tomorrow, it would demand more.

And he, like all the others, would obey.

Joras woke before his notification buzzed, his body trained by the demands of the system. Sleep had not been rest so much as a period of suspended awareness, his mind still calculating, still anticipating. The factory had imprinted itself onto him. Even in the quiet of his pod, his muscles twitched as if they were still sorting, still reaching, still moving in the unrelenting rhythm Capitalschism had set. He barely noticed the dim, blue glow of the city filtering in through the pod's filtration vents. Everything outside the factory was beginning to feel like a holding pattern, a limbo that only existed so he could return to work. The distinction between labor and existence was thinning.

The moment his wrist vibrated, he was already moving, pulling on his uniform, syncing his credentials, stepping onto the transit line. There were no choices in these moments, no opportunity to pause or reconsider. The path was predetermined, like a conveyor belt for workers, moving them from their pods to their assignments with the same efficiency as the factory moved its packages. He scanned his wrist at the entrance, the turnstile sliding open with a hollow chime. His queue updated in real-time, slotting him into a new role, this time, inventory reconciliation. Another adjustment. Another reassignment. There was no pattern to it, no consistency. The factory was dynamic, shifting workers around like chess pieces, adjusting them based on fluctuating demand. What seemed arbitrary was, in fact, finely tuned, an invisible hand deciding, moment by moment, where each unit of labor could be best extracted.

He followed the illuminated path, feeling the tightness in his limbs, the familiar stiffness that would not fade. The body adapted to pain, but it did not erase it. His station came into view, a sprawling area lined with conveyor feeds, autonomous scanners, and sorting bays. He was to inspect flagged packages, check for discrepancies in weight and dimensions, verify their destinations. It sounded simple. Nothing was simple here. Every action was timed, logged, evaluated. There was no room for second-guessing, no space for thought beyond what was immediately in front of him. The first package arrived within seconds, sliding into position with a mechanical whir. He scanned the barcode. The screen flashed a readout, expected weight, expected contents, expected location. He checked the physical weight against the listed metric, confirmed, sent it forward. The next one appeared. Then another. Then another.

Joras had learned by now that the system did not care about accuracy the way a human might. It did not operate on the principle of getting things right, of ensuring each package was perfectly accounted for. It operated on efficiency. The target was not correctness, but speed, maintaining an output high enough to meet the demands of an economy that never stopped consuming. The system tolerated a small margin of error if it meant processing more orders. But it did not tolerate delays. If he hesitated too long, the conveyor would flag him for inaction. If he spent too much time verifying a discrepancy, his rating would drop. The best workers weren't the most precise. They were the fastest.

The factory pulsed around him, an organism larger than any single person. The machines adjusted seamlessly, optimizing their functions, their patterns, their distribution of tasks. Joras moved within it, absorbed, another component in its endless recalibration. There was something deeply unsettling about it, not just the work itself, but the way the factory seemed to think, to learn. It was not alive, not in the way people were, but it had intent. It was evolving, adapting, fine-tuning itself with every passing moment. It studied its workers, analyzed their weaknesses, recalculated its demands to push them further. And just as they learned to navigate it, it learned to extract more from them. It was not cruel, not in the way an overseer with a whip might be. But it was relentless. And it never, ever stopped.

His wrist buzzed. A red alert flashed on his interface. *Performance Warning: Below Expected Efficiency Threshold.*

His breath caught. He had barely noticed the drop, barely registered the moment when his pace had slowed. It had only been seconds. Maybe a minute. Had he hesitated too long on a package? Had his movements been sluggish? The system would not tell him. It did not explain. It only measured. And it had decided he was slipping.

A cold wave passed through him, something deeper than fear, more profound than anxiety. He could not afford a second warning. Too many in a single cycle would trigger a full evaluation, which could lead to suspension, which could lead to deactivation. And deactivation, losing access to the system, was the same as being erased. There was no appeal. No second chances. Once the system decided you were inefficient, you were gone. The factory did not carry dead weight.
He corrected immediately, forcing his hands to move faster, scanning, weighing, confirming at a pace just short of reckless. The red notification faded. The system was watching. He was regaining favor.

Break notifications came and went. Five minutes, precisely calculated, just enough to keep him functional. He did not waste them. He hydrated. He reset. He did not linger. The moment his wrist buzzed, he returned to work without hesitation. He had learned. He understood the rules now.

The shift stretched on, folding time into a seamless loop of labor, reaction, adjustment. The outside world was meaningless here. There was only the factory, only the process, only the next package and the one after that. When the final notification came, *Shift Completed. Exit Route Assigned,* he felt no relief, only the lingering tension of knowing he would return.

Outside, the city gleamed, indifferent to those who powered it. Workers spilled into the transit lanes, filtering back into their pods, their temporary housing, their places of waiting. Joras moved among them, another nameless figure in the flow, his wrist buzzing with his updated performance rating. It was acceptable. For now.

He boarded the transport, barely feeling the movement as it carried him away from the factory, away but not free. His body still anticipated the next notification, still braced for the next demand. His mind still sorted, still scanned, still processed. He had been conditioned.

As the transit line wove through the city, he caught glimpses of others outside the system. The ones who had been deactivated, whose profiles had been erased from the workforce. They gathered in clusters beneath overpasses, lingered in unlit corners, waiting. The city did not remove them, not immediately. It let them fade on their own, drift toward irrelevance, disappear. A silent warning to those still within the system. Keep up. Stay useful. Do not slow down.

His pod was waiting, precisely as he had left it. A temporary shelter, not a home, never a home. The walls pulsed softly, adjusting the temperature to the company's recommended sleep conditions. The system was still watching, still measuring. It would track his rest, his recovery, his readiness. If he woke unrested, it would know. If he did not sync properly before his shift, it would know.

He sat on the edge of the sleeping pad, staring at the projected interface on the wall. His metrics, his efficiency curve, his projected workload for tomorrow. The numbers flickered, unreadable in his exhaustion. He could not stop thinking about the alert, the warning, the way the system had registered his hesitation and adjusted accordingly.

Somewhere, deep inside Capitalschism, the factory had already begun recalculating. It had measured his output, factored in his fatigue, assessed his ability to maintain pace. It had adjusted his thresholds, refined its expectations, determined how much more it could take from him.

Tomorrow, it would push him harder.

And he, like all the others, would comply.

3
Algorithms and Chains

Ona stared at the numbers shifting on her screen, watching them recalculate, adjust, and recalibrate with each passing second, yet never in her favor. It was a cruel rhythm, the algorithm's way of pretending there was some pattern she could master, some logic she could decipher if she only worked harder, moved faster, optimized better. But she knew now, there was no winning this game. The system always won. And it was designed that way.

Her morning had started with promise, or at least the illusion of it. A flood of microtasks filled her queue, simple, repetitive jobs, each promising a tiny payout if completed fast enough. Data entry, survey participation, image classification, voice transcription. The work came in waves, an endless, shifting tide, always temporary, always just enough to make her think she was progressing, even as her balance remained frustratingly low. She had trained herself to react instantly, clicking before the best jobs could vanish, snatching up the highest-paying tasks before someone else could claim them. But it never mattered.

At first, she had believed in the logic of it. The forums were filled with strategies, advice from other workers who claimed they had cracked the code, found the patterns, learned the secret to gaming the system. Work during surge hours. Accept every task. Maintain a high response rate. Avoid rejecting jobs or the algorithm would deprioritize you. But even they admitted that no strategy worked forever. The system was always learning, adapting, adjusting its payouts in ways that ensured workers never made too much, never got ahead, never became anything more than an expendable part of the machine.

She accepted another task, data transcription, estimated pay: $3.50 for 22 minutes of work. It was better than most. She typed quickly, efficiently, her fingers moving with practiced precision. The words on the screen blurred into nothingness, fragments of conversations, random strings of text, meaningless snippets extracted from surveillance feeds or AI-generated dialogue models. She didn't know who they belonged to or where they would end up. It wasn't her job to know. It was her job to process, to extract value where the system had deemed value extractable. She finished in 19 minutes. A notification flashed.

Earnings adjusted: $2.80.

Her stomach clenched. The task had listed a fixed rate. She checked the breakdown. A penalty for early completion, classified as *probable automation.* The system had determined that she had finished too quickly, meaning she must have used an AI tool to assist her. The assumption was incorrect, of course. She had simply worked efficiently. But the system did not trust efficiency. It punished it.

She pressed her fingers into her temples, forcing herself to breathe, to stay calm. There was no appeals process. There was no one to call, no support line to dispute the decision. The system had ruled, and that was the end of it.

She checked her daily total. It was lower than expected. Lower than the same amount of work had paid yesterday. This, too, was by design. The longer a worker remained on the platform, the less they earned. The algorithm tracked their behavior, identified patterns, marked them as *reliable.* And the moment the system determined a worker was dependent on its wages, the downward adjustments began. New users received better offers, higher payouts, enticing bonuses. But once they were trapped, once they had no other choice, the numbers dropped.

She had watched it happen to Joras. He had considered quitting his delivery job last month, fed up with the hidden costs, the rental fees, the insurance deductions, the shifting pay scales that made it impossible to predict how much he would actually take home. The moment he hesitated, his app flooded him with high-paying offers, tempting him to stay. He had accepted a few, thinking maybe the system was rewarding him for loyalty. But within days, the pay had dropped again, settling back into the barely livable range that kept him running just fast enough to survive.

A notification pulsed. Survey opportunity. Five-minute task. Payment: $0.45.

Ona declined. Not worth the effort. But the moment she rejected the offer, her queue emptied.

Her breath caught. She had read about this. The system had noticed her hesitation. It would deprioritize her now, flag her as *selective,* reduce the frequency of job offers. The only way to maintain a steady flow of work was to accept everything. But accepting everything meant working for nothing.

Her hand trembled slightly as she checked their balance. It was lower than it should have been. A new deduction, service fees, processing charges, an *adjustment* to their rental rate. Ona exhaled sharply. The numbers were slipping faster than she could correct them.

Miklas stirred in the corner, shifting in his sleep, his small fingers curling into the blanket. Ona watched him for a moment, her frustration hardening into something heavier, something close to grief. She had told herself, when they first arrived, that this was temporary. That this was only a stepping stone, a necessary struggle before they found stability. But the city did not allow for stability. The moment you thought you had gained ground, the system shifted, the numbers recalculated, the costs increased. There was no climbing out. There was only running in place.

Her device buzzed again. Another task.

She accepted.

She worked.

She obeyed.

Hours passed. The numbers climbed, but never enough. A deduction here, a penalty there. A game she could never win.

Joras returned late, his movements slow, his face drawn. He sat beside her in silence, his body heavy with exhaustion. She did not ask about his day. She already knew.

"We're slipping," she said finally, her voice barely above a whisper.

Joras exhaled, rubbing a hand over his face. "I know."

Silence stretched between them.

"There has to be something else," Ona said.

Joras let out a hollow laugh. "Like what?"

Ona didn't answer.

Because she didn't know.

Because the system had already taken the answer from them.

Joras leaned forward, resting his head in his hands. Ona watched him, the man she had built a life with, the man she had once dreamed beside, planned beside. She saw the weight pressing down on him, the same quiet resignation creeping into his voice that she felt in her own.

She wanted to tell him they could figure it out. That they would find a way through. But she couldn't make herself say the words. Because something inside her, something buried deep but growing stronger with each passing day, was starting to believe it wasn't true.

Miklas stirred again, shifting onto his side, murmuring something inaudible in his sleep. Ona reached over, tucking the blanket around him, smoothing his hair with gentle fingers.

Joras watched her. "I used to think we were smarter than this," he said.

Ona didn't look up. "Smarter than what?"

"This." He gestured vaguely, his hand sweeping over the tiny, suffocating space, the dim glow of their balance sheet flickering on the wall, the weight of the system pressing down on them from every direction. "I thought we'd find a way to beat it."

Ona let out a slow breath. "It doesn't matter how smart we are."

Joras was quiet for a long moment. Then, finally, he said, "No. It doesn't."

They sat there, side by side, the weight of unspoken truths settling between them.

Outside, the city continued, its machines humming, its systems recalculating, optimizing, refining. Somewhere, deep within its algorithms, their futures were already being rewritten. Their work scores. Their debt ratios. Their probabilities of success or failure. The system was preparing for another day, another cycle, another round of labor to be extracted.

And they, like all the others, would comply.

The notices came in waves, quiet intrusions that altered the fabric of their reality without ceremony. At first, they were small, a minor rent adjustment here, an increase in service fees there. Barely noticeable. The kind of fluctuations that could be explained away, ignored even, if one didn't look too closely. But Ona had learned to look closely. She had trained herself to see the patterns, to anticipate the adjustments before they hit, to run the numbers in her head faster than the system could update. Yet no matter how fast she worked, no matter how much she optimized, the gap between their income and their expenses widened with each passing week.

The most recent increase came in the form of a recalibrated housing rate, an "optimization" of their rental contract, adjusted for *real-time demand metrics*. The city's justification was simple: more workers were arriving, more people needed housing, and scarcity justified a price hike. Ona knew better. There was no scarcity. The rental pods were mass-produced, identical in every way, stacked into endless grids that stretched beyond the horizon. The supply was infinite. But the system did not care about supply. It cared about control. About maintaining pressure. About ensuring that no one ever felt secure enough to stop running.

She stared at the notification, her mind cycling through calculations, looking for a way to absorb the new cost. But there was nothing left to absorb. They had already cut everything that could be cut. There were no luxuries, no excesses. The city had refined their lives down to necessity, and now it was taking pieces of the necessity as well.

Ona checked her earnings, running a projection in her head. If she worked longer hours, if she took on more low-paying tasks, if she pushed just a little harder, maybe they could stay afloat. But the numbers didn't work. The algorithm had already marked her as dependent. It had begun adjusting her payouts downward, reducing her earning potential as soon as it determined she was too reliant to leave. She had known this was coming. She had read about it in the forums, had seen it happen to others. But knowing didn't make it any easier to endure.

Joras had stopped tracking the numbers. He didn't want to see them anymore. He worked, he came home, he ate just enough to keep moving, and then he worked again. Ona had tried to talk to him about the adjustments, about the fact that their debt balance had increased even though they were making regular payments, about the predatory interest structures that made it impossible to pay anything down. He had listened, nodded, and then left for another shift.

They had stopped talking about the future. That was the first thing the system took from them, not money, not stability, but the ability to imagine anything beyond survival.

Miklas needed shoes. That was the thing that finally broke her. It was such a small thing, such an ordinary need. But when she looked at the marketplace listings and saw the price, she felt something inside her fracture. The cheapest pair was still too expensive. She thought about delaying the purchase, about waiting for a sale, about stretching his current pair just a little longer. But she had seen the way he curled his toes inside them, the way he tried not to complain. He was learning the unspoken rules of their world, the quiet calculus of sacrifice, the instinct to endure discomfort in silence.

She closed the marketplace app and exhaled. "Maybe next week," she muttered, not realizing she had said it aloud.

Joras looked up from where he sat, sorting through his queue of available shifts. "What?"

Ona kept her eyes on the screen. "Miklas needs new shoes."

Joras rubbed his face, his fingers pressing into his temples. "How bad?"

"They don't fit anymore."

A silence stretched between them, heavy and suffocating. Ona could see the tension settling into Joras' shoulders, the slow build of frustration with nowhere to go.

"Then we'll get them," he said finally, but his voice was empty, hollow.

She wanted to tell him it was fine. That they could wait. That Miklas could manage a little longer. But she didn't. Because it wasn't fine. And he shouldn't have to wait.

Joras stood abruptly, grabbing his coat.

"Where are you going?"

"To get another shift."

Ona felt something sharp twist in her chest. "You just got home."

He didn't answer.

She stood as well, moving in front of him before she realized what she was doing. "Joras, you can't keep doing this."

His jaw clenched. "What do you want me to do, Ona? Huh? Tell me. Because I don't see another option."

"There has to be another way."

"Like what?"

She opened her mouth, but nothing came.

Joras exhaled sharply, running a hand over his face. He looked at her, and for the first time, she saw something in his eyes that scared her more than anger, more than frustration. Resignation.

"This is how it works," he said quietly. "This is how they keep us moving."

Ona knew he was right. The system wasn't just about money. It was about exhaustion. About ensuring that no one had the time to think, to plan, to fight. It was about breaking people down into manageable, predictable inputs.

Joras turned away, grabbing his work device, checking the available shifts. Ona sat back down, staring at the flickering numbers on her own screen, at the queue that had started refilling, at the pending deductions that would hit their balance in the next cycle.

Miklas stirred in his sleep, shifting against the blanket, his face relaxed, untouched by any of this.

Ona wanted to believe it would be different for him. That they would find a way to give him something better.

But she was beginning to understand the truth.

No one escaped the system.

They just learned how to survive inside it.

She picked up her device. And kept working.

Joras had never felt like this before, not exactly. The exhaustion, the strain, the quiet terror of watching numbers move against him no matter how hard he worked, all of that had become normal, a dull, persistent background hum that never left his body. But this, this creeping, suffocating weight in his chest, this constant knot of tension between his shoulders, this sense that every breath he took was being measured and calculated and somehow counted against him, it was new. Or maybe it had always been there, and he was only just now recognizing it for what it was.

Ona had stopped trying to talk to him about the numbers. Not because they didn't matter anymore, but because they mattered too much. Because talking about them only confirmed what they both already knew: there was no fixing this. The math would never work in their favor. The system was designed to keep them just solvent enough to keep moving, to make sure they never collapsed completely but also never got far enough ahead to stop running.

Still, she tracked everything. Late at night, when Miklas was asleep and Joras was too tired to do anything but stare blankly at the walls, she would sit with her device, scrolling through the ledgers, watching the balances shift. The rental rate had increased again, another "optimization" to reflect demand. The energy surcharge had risen despite no change in usage. The microloan they had taken for their initial housing deposit had adjusted its repayment terms, shortening the period and raising the interest. The food subscription had applied a new premium for *priority delivery*, a service they had never requested.

It didn't matter how many hours they worked. The system would always find a way to take more.

Joras spent his days cycling between warehouse shifts and delivery contracts. He had stopped bothering to plan his schedule in advance. There was no point. The system adjusted his offers dynamically, based on demand, based on his past work history, based on whatever hidden metrics it used to determine how much pressure to apply. If he worked too many hours, his per-task pay rate would drop. If he worked too few, he would be flagged as *unreliable*, reducing his access to higher-paying jobs. If he tried to game the system, taking long breaks between shifts to reset his efficiency rating, the algorithm would penalize him in other ways, fewer job offers, lower bonuses, subtle reductions in available work that would force him to accept worse contracts just to keep up.

There was no strategy. No way to stay ahead. The system always knew.

And now, the tension between him and Ona was shifting into something heavier, something harder to ignore. It wasn't the kind of tension that erupted into shouting matches or heated arguments. It was quieter than that, more insidious. It was in the way they moved around each other in their tiny rental pod, careful not to touch, careful not to speak unless absolutely necessary. It was in the way Ona stared at her device long after she should have gone to sleep, in the way Joras left earlier and earlier in the morning, coming home later and later at night. It was in the way neither of them acknowledged how much harder things were getting, as though speaking it aloud would make it worse, would force them to confront the reality that they were no longer trying to improve their situation, they were merely trying to survive it.

They still touched, sometimes. Still reached for each other in the dark, their bodies pressed together in silent desperation, as if trying to remember a time when they had been something other than tired, something other than functionaries in a system that refused to let them rest. But even that was slipping away. The exhaustion had made them strangers. Joras felt it most acutely in the moments before sleep, when Ona's breathing should have been slow and even, but instead remained tense, shallow, as if she were bracing herself against the next unexpected cost, the next algorithmic punishment, the next recalibration of their lives in a direction neither of them had chosen.

He felt it in the small moments, in the way Ona's fingers tightened around her device when another unexpected deduction hit their balance. The way she exhaled a little too slowly, a little too carefully, when she saw the numbers. The way her voice had grown quieter, her responses shorter, as if conserving energy for the battle she fought every day against an opponent that couldn't be seen, couldn't be touched, couldn't be beaten. He watched as she scrolled through endless task lists, her eyes scanning for something, anything, that paid enough to justify the time it took. He heard her breath catch in frustration when a task disappeared just as she was about to accept it, snatched away by someone faster, someone more desperate. He saw the way she clenched her jaw when a completed job suddenly paid less than promised, when her earnings were quietly adjusted downward by a system that never had to explain itself.

They had always been partners. Even when things were hard, they had faced it together. But now, they weren't facing it together at all. They were simply enduring in parallel, each too consumed by their own struggle to fully see the other. Their exhaustion was no longer just a condition of their labor, it was their existence. Even in the moments they shared, the fleeting pockets of time that belonged to them alone, there was no relief. There was only the shadow of the next shift, the weight of the next deduction, the knowledge that nothing would ever be enough.

The shift came one evening, though in reality, it had been coming for a long time.

Joras had pushed himself too hard that day. He had taken back-to-back shifts, rushing from one warehouse to another, skipping breaks, ignoring the protests of his body. He had ignored the flashing warnings on his device, *fatigue detected, dehydration risk, muscle strain warning.* He had ignored everything except the numbers, except the sinking balance in their account, except the quiet fear of watching the system pull them further under, one transaction at a time. His fingers ached from gripping delivery handles too tightly, his back throbbed from lifting improperly balanced loads, his legs burned from cycling across the city without stopping. But he couldn't stop. He couldn't afford to.

By the time he got home, he could barely think. His body ached, his hands trembled from overuse. He dropped onto the sleeping mat beside Ona, exhaling sharply. The synthetic surface conformed to his shape, sensing his weight, adjusting to "maximize rest efficiency." A feature meant to ensure workers remained functional, not comfortable.

She didn't look up from her device.

"You're late," she said.

Joras let out a dry laugh. "No such thing as late when there's no schedule."

Ona's fingers tightened around the device. "You can't keep doing this."

Joras closed his eyes. He was too tired for this conversation. Too tired to tell her what she already knew. "What choice do I have?"

Ona's breath hitched, and when she spoke again, there was something raw in her voice. "Joras, we're falling apart."

He opened his eyes.

She wasn't talking about their finances.
Joras sat up, rubbing his face. His body ached. Everything ached. "I know."

Ona stared at him for a long moment. "Then we need to stop pretending this is sustainable."

Joras wanted to argue. Wanted to tell her they could fix it, that they could work harder, plan better, find a way through. But the words felt hollow, even in his own mind. He had spent so much time convincing himself that all they needed was endurance, that if they could just hold on long enough, something would shift in their favor. But it never had. And it never would.

Ona turned the device toward him. "I've been looking into other options."

Joras frowned. "What kind of options?"

She hesitated. "There are places outside the city. Smaller communities. They run on different systems. Not entirely disconnected, but not as controlled as here."

Joras stared at the screen. The idea felt impossible. Leaving meant uncertainty. It meant giving up everything they had worked for, abandoning the infrastructure that had kept them alive, even if that same infrastructure was suffocating them. It meant leaving behind the only way of life they had known. But staying meant more of this. More shifts. More penalties. More months of barely treading water. It meant watching Ona break herself against a system that would never let her win. It meant watching Miklas grow up in a world where exhaustion was inherited, where survival was a full-time job.

And yet…

For the first time in as long as he could remember, he felt something other than exhaustion. A spark of something he couldn't quite name.

Hope?

No. Not yet.

But something close.

He looked at Ona, really looked at her, at the dark circles under her eyes, at the way her shoulders slumped with exhaustion, at the quiet determination in her expression. She had already made her choice. She was just waiting for him to make his.

"We can't just leave," he said, though the words were already losing their conviction.

Ona held his gaze. "Can't we?"

Joras exhaled. He didn't have an answer.

But for the first time in a long time, he was willing to ask the question.

4
The Greed Virus

Joras had known for a long time that his body would fail before the system did. He had felt it coming in the small ways, the deep, persistent ache in his knees, the stiffness in his back that no amount of stretching could undo, the way his hands would sometimes tremble after too many consecutive shifts, as if they were slowly detaching from his will. He had seen it happen to others, the way they moved slower over time, the way the warning signs accumulated like rust in a machine that was never meant to stop. And yet, when it finally happened to him, it still felt like a betrayal.

The shift had been like any other. A route assignment had come in overnight, the payout calculated in real-time, fluctuating as more workers accepted or declined. He had taken it immediately, early-morning slots sometimes paid marginally better, and he was still trying to offset the last unexpected rent hike. It was a heavy route, multiple packages, some flagged as urgent, which meant the system would be tracking his speed more closely, recalibrating his performance score with every stop.

He had been careful. Even exhausted, even barely conscious, he had trained himself to move efficiently, to match the rhythm the system demanded. But that day, something went wrong.

The package wasn't supposed to be that heavy. The manifest had labeled it as *standard*, but when he lifted it, he felt an immediate shift in his lower back, a deep, unnatural pull, like something inside him had been twisted in the wrong direction. He barely had time to process it before the pain hit, sharp and searing, radiating through his spine and down his leg. He dropped to one knee, his breath catching in his throat. The package slipped from his hands, landing hard against the pavement.

His device vibrated, *delivery incomplete*. A warning flashed: *Package mishandled. Performance rating adjusted.*

Joras clenched his jaw, forcing himself to breathe through the pain. He reached for the package again, slower this time, using what little strength he could summon. His vision blurred. He could feel the algorithm recalculating in real-time, flagging his delays, adjusting his metrics, deciding in cold, detached precision that he was no longer meeting expectations.

The rest of the route was a blur of agony. Every step sent shocks of pain through his body, but stopping wasn't an option. The system did not acknowledge injury. He had no supervisor to call, no one to approve a break. If he abandoned the route, his rating would plummet. If he took too long, future job offers would be reduced. The only path forward was through.

By the time he finished, his body was drenched in sweat. His fingers fumbled with the final delivery confirmation, his breath coming in short, ragged bursts. The system responded instantly, *Route complete. Performance logged. Future recommendations updated.*

No acknowledgment of his pain. No adjustment for the injury. No option to report what had happened. He was a data point, nothing more, his suffering noted only as a momentary inefficiency in an otherwise optimized process.

The walk home was unbearable. Each step was a battle between gravity and endurance, between the sharp, electric pain in his spine and the knowledge that stopping wouldn't change anything. He imagined what it would feel like to collapse, to let his body give in, to become another nameless worker who had simply failed to keep up. He had seen them before, the ones who dropped in transit lanes, who froze mid-task, who sat slumped against walls with empty eyes, waiting for the inevitable. He had always wondered what happened to them after. He had never wanted to find out.

The pod was too quiet when he entered. Ona was working, Miklas still asleep, the soft glow of the interface the only source of movement in the room. He lowered himself onto the sleeping mat, biting back a groan as the pain flared again. His hands shook as he checked his device, navigating to the benefits page.

Healthcare support available. Eligibility based on performance metrics.

His chest tightened. He scrolled further, reading the fine print. *Injury verification required. Claims may affect job availability. Processing times vary. Support approval subject to system evaluation.*

Joras exhaled slowly. There it was. The thing they never said outright, but that every worker knew. The *support* was a performance penalty in disguise. Reporting an injury would trigger a recalculation of his work potential, an adjustment to his task offers, a quiet marking in the system that he was *high-risk.* He would receive fewer jobs. The payout rates would drop. His reliability score would decline.

And then, when he had been drained of usefulness, when the numbers had dipped below whatever threshold the system deemed acceptable, the offers would stop altogether.

It was a cycle he had seen before. The system did not fire workers. It simply phased them out. A gradual reduction in opportunities, a slow deprivation of income, a quiet, calculated erasure.

He could report the injury. Or he could pretend it wasn't there.

A movement in the corner of his vision. Ona, watching him.

"You're hurt," she said softly.

Joras forced himself to sit up straighter, gritting his teeth against the pain. "It's nothing."

Ona's eyes flickered to his hands, still trembling, to the way he held himself too still, too carefully. "Joras."

He exhaled. "If I report it, they'll cut my work offers."

Ona's face remained impassive, but he could see the tension in her jaw, the quiet anger pressing against the edges of her exhaustion. "That's not how it's supposed to work."

Joras laughed, though there was no humor in it. "Supposed to?" He gestured to the interface, still glowing softly beside them. "None of this is supposed to work this way. But it does."

She sat down beside him, pressing her palms together, staring at the floor. He could see the calculations running behind her eyes, the same ones he had gone through, what they could afford to lose, how much risk they could take, what the system would allow.

"What do you want to do?" she asked finally.

Joras let his head fall back against the wall, staring at the ceiling. What did he want to do? He wanted to stop. To rest. To exist in a way that didn't feel like a constant negotiation between survival and collapse. But none of that was an option.
I'll keep working," he said.

Ona didn't argue.

But she didn't agree, either.

The next day, Joras forced himself out the door. Every movement was agony. The system, as expected, had adjusted. His work offers had already begun to shift, shorter routes, lower payouts, the algorithm testing his capacity, waiting to see if he would break. He moved carefully, slowly, each step a careful negotiation with the pain radiating through his body.

At a stoplight, he saw another worker slump against a wall, his eyes vacant, his body unmoving. A drone hovered nearby, scanning, logging. No one stopped. No one intervened.

Joras turned away.

That night, as he lay in bed, pain still radiating through his spine, he thought about the notices that had started appearing in their messages, pre-approved credit offers, short-term loans with *worker-friendly repayment plans*, emergency funds available *instantly*. He had ignored them before. But now, as the pain made every breath feel like a debt being collected, he understood why people took them.

The system had already anticipated this. It had already accounted for him. It had already prepared for the moment he would need to borrow just to keep going.

The trap had been set long before he ever stepped inside it.

And now, there was no way out.

The messages started appearing almost immediately. Joras hadn't even fully processed the extent of his injury before the system began its next phase of engagement: the recovery pipeline, the illusion of help. His device pulsed with notifications, special offers for short-term financial assistance, pre-approved emergency credit, exclusive worker protection plans with *instant* approval. Each one framed with the same neutral, vaguely supportive language. Each one a carefully calculated pressure point. The system had already anticipated this moment. It had already known he would need money before he had even admitted it to himself.

He ignored the first wave, swiping them away as he lay in the dark, back burning, muscles locked in unnatural tension. He would sleep, he told himself. He would recover. He would not let the system win. But sleep never came, only the pulsing of his device in the corner of the room, lighting up in rhythmic intervals, offering its quiet assurances. *You're not alone. Help is available.*

By morning, the numbers were worse. Ona sat on the sleeping mat, scanning their balance, her face unreadable but her silence heavy with meaning. Joras didn't ask, he already knew. Another deduction. A recalculated debt. A new cost justified by an *updated risk assessment.* The system always adjusted for instability.

It had detected his reduced output, reclassified his financial tier, applied interest adjustments accordingly. He hadn't even missed a full day of work, but already, the consequences were unfolding.

Ona finally spoke without looking up. "The food credits didn't renew."

Joras clenched his jaw. "Why?"

"They moved us into a new bracket."

He exhaled sharply. The city's *nutritional assistance* was based on work metrics, another performance-based benefit that fluctuated with demand. The less you worked, the less you ate. Or rather, the more you worked, the more access you had to *affordable* food. Workers who fell below a certain threshold could still buy meals, but without the subsidies, the costs were exponential. The same pre-packaged calorie rations that had been manageable last week were now double the price.

Ona scrolled through the adjustments, fingers tightening around the device. "I'll stretch it," she murmured. "Miklas eats first."

Joras didn't argue.

Miklas always ate first.

That afternoon, a physical letter arrived. A rare thing. An official-looking envelope, slipped under the door while they weren't home, as if hand-delivered. No stamp. No sender.

Joras opened it with numb fingers, scanning the contents without reading at first. The words blurred, formal and distant, paragraphs designed to create the illusion of choice while removing all actual agency. A *limited-time opportunity* to refinance their debts. A *customized* repayment plan tailored to *workers in transition*. Access to exclusive *stability loans* meant for *valuable members of the workforce*.

He gritted his teeth, forcing himself to read it again, to absorb the details. The offer was clear: a lump sum deposited immediately into their account, enough to clear overdue balances, enough to reset the spiraling interest rates, enough to give them the illusion of a clean slate. The terms, however, were predatory. Interest tied to work output, meaning payments fluctuated based on their ability to keep pace. Penalties for missed shifts. Late fees applied *dynamically* based on *market conditions*. A repayment structure designed to keep them locked in permanent obligation.

He tossed the letter onto the floor. "They know."

Ona looked up.

"They always know." He gestured to the paper, shaking his head. "They don't offer these loans to people who are stable. They wait until you start drowning. Then they throw you a rope that tightens around your neck."

Ona said nothing for a long time.

Joras rubbed his temples, exhaustion weighing heavier than ever. "We don't take it."

"We might have to."

He stared at her. "Ona—"

"I'm just saying," she interrupted, voice measured, careful. "I'm not saying today. But if something else happens—"

She didn't finish the sentence. She didn't have to.

Joras exhaled, pressing his hands over his face. He hated that she was right.

The system had made sure of it.

That evening, Ona combed through the expenses again, recalculating, adjusting, cutting where she could. She stopped eating full meals, rationing portions even tighter than before. Joras noticed the way she portioned Miklas' food carefully, measuring everything, calculating how many more days she could stretch their dwindling credits before she had to make a choice. He noticed how her own portions shrank day by day, how she turned away when he looked at her plate.

By the end of the week, the weight of desperation was tangible. Ona's body was slowing down. Her skin looked paler in the artificial light of the pod, her movements more deliberate, her energy conserved. Joras felt the guilt clawing at his chest, but he knew what she would say if he brought it up. *Miklas eats first.* Always.

Miklas, who had stopped asking for things. Who had learned, somehow, the unspoken rules of their world, the quiet mathematics of deprivation. Joras had once promised himself that no matter what, he would protect his son from this. But the system had other plans.

He remembered the shoes. How Ona had hesitated before mentioning them. How she had already known they couldn't afford them, had already done the math before speaking. How Joras had left that night, determined to find another shift, to stretch their limits just a little further. And yet, despite everything, the shoes still had not been bought.

He imagined Miklas in school, surrounded by other children, some as poor as him, others who still had the illusion of comfort, who still lived in homes where food was plentiful and shoes were replaced when they wore out. He imagined his son curling his toes inside the too-tight fabric, trying not to notice, trying not to care.

Joras clenched his fists. He felt something inside him snap.

He stood, pacing the length of the pod, too restless to sit, too angry to be still. Ona watched him but said nothing.

"We can't live like this," he muttered.

Ona closed her eyes. "I know."

"No, I mean—" He stopped, turning to face her fully. "We *really* can't. Not just because it's hard. Because it's *designed* this way. They push us until we break. Then they offer a way out that only digs us deeper. They *need* us to be desperate."

Ona exhaled. "I know."

Joras ran a hand over his face, his heart pounding. The walls of the pod felt smaller, suffocating. The entire city felt like a mechanism built to consume them, to extract every ounce of energy, every possible unit of productivity, and then discard them when there was nothing left.

Miklas shuffled in his sleep, shifting in the dim light.

Ona's eyes softened. "We still have choices," she murmured. "Not good ones. But we do."

Joras looked at her.

Ona reached for her device. Opened the encrypted messages she had been keeping secret until now. The ones she had been reading late at night, after Joras had collapsed into exhausted sleep.

She turned the screen toward him. A name, a location, a possibility.

Not a solution. But something close.

"We need to decide," she whispered.

Joras looked at the screen, at the quiet offering of escape, at the impossibility of it.

And for the first time in weeks, he felt something other than despair.

It wasn't hope.

Not yet.

But it was the beginning of something else.
Ona knew she had learned to ration before she had ever made the conscious choice to do so. It had started in small ways, adjusting meal portions, stretching supplies, making do with less while telling herself it was temporary. The food credits had once seemed stable enough, a quiet assurance that no matter how hard things became, there would always be something left at the end of the day. But now, she understood that stability had never been real. It had been a carefully designed illusion, a variable the system could manipulate at will, adjusting availability, increasing costs, shifting requirements. The moment they had fallen below a certain threshold, the balance had recalibrated.
Nutritional assistance adjusted due to performance decline.

She didn't tell Joras everything. There was no need. He already knew in the way she portioned Miklas' food first, in the way she handed him his own plate with a small, forced smile, in the way she distracted him when he noticed she wasn't eating as much. The hunger wasn't immediate, not yet, not the kind that left the body weak and shaking, not the kind that blurred vision and slowed thoughts. But it would be, eventually.

Joras had started watching her more closely, noticing the way her movements slowed, the way her energy dipped just slightly more with each passing day. She had become precise in her stillness, conserving herself, calculating her own survival the same way she calculated their remaining funds. There was no excess, no indulgence, no moment wasted. She drank more water when she was hungry. She chewed slower when she ate. It was a science, and she had perfected it.

Miklas, at least, was still too young to fully see it. He had learned not to ask for things, had absorbed the quiet lessons without being told. Ona had once thought children had to be taught sacrifice. Now she realized they learned it on their own.

Joras tried to compensate. He took longer shifts, ignored his own pain, ran himself into the ground in a way that made Ona sick to watch. She wanted to stop him, to tell him to slow down, but there was nothing else to be done. The system would take everything they gave, and they had no choice but to keep offering themselves up.

The messages from the lenders became more aggressive. The polite formality of the first wave had been replaced with more direct language, *Immediate action required. Urgent debt restructuring available. Missed this opportunity? Don't worry, we have another.* Ona deleted most of them before Joras could see them. He already carried too much.

One evening, after another long day of struggling to keep pace with a system designed to move just slightly faster than human endurance allowed, Joras came home with something in his hand. A package. A plain, non-descript bag, but Ona knew what it was before he said anything.

Shoes.

For Miklas.

She looked at them, then at him. "Where did you get these?"

Joras sat down heavily, exhaling as if the act of sitting took more energy than it should. "Picked up an extra route," he said, not meeting her eyes. "Delivery incentives were high today."

Ona didn't believe him. The incentives were never high enough to justify something like this. Not anymore. But she didn't argue. She only ran her hands over the shoes, tracing the stitching, the soft material. They were good ones. Not the cheapest available. Not the kind that would fall apart in a month.

Miklas was already asleep. She would give them to him in the morning.

She set them aside and turned back to Joras. His face was drawn, exhausted, the deep lines in his forehead heavier than usual. She didn't ask how much he had pushed himself for this, how much deeper into exhaustion he had sunk to make this happen.

She only reached for his hand, fingers brushing against his, a silent thank you.

Joras exhaled again, closing his eyes.

They sat together in the dim glow of the interface, the weight of survival pressing in around them.

Outside, the city continued its endless cycle. The system recalculated. The algorithms adjusted. Somewhere, in a quiet database, their desperation had been logged, analyzed, prepared for the next phase.

They didn't need to discuss it. They both knew.

The greed virus had already infected every part of their lives.

And there was no cure.

5
The Gilded Age Returns

Joras had stopped thinking of their pod as home a long time ago. It had always been a temporary structure, a waystation rather than a destination, but in recent months, it had begun to feel more like a holding cell. The walls had never been meant to comfort, only to contain, and every change the system had made, from rent adjustments to resource rationing, had been another step toward pushing them out. The system had a way of moving them incrementally, of tightening the noose so gradually that by the time the final tug came, there was nothing left to fight against. Just the inevitability of their relocation, calculated and predetermined long before they received the notice.

The eviction notice had arrived with the same detached efficiency as everything else. No dramatic warning, no human voice delivering the news, just a quiet update to their account balance. *Your current residence no longer meets eligibility requirements. Alternative housing has been secured for your continued employment.* It was phrased as an opportunity, as if this wasn't an expulsion but an adjustment for their benefit. The language was always carefully chosen. Words like *opportunity*, *optimization*, *streamlining*, and *realignment* softened the edges of what was, at its core, a system designed to extract until there was nothing left.

Joras and Ona had known it was coming. The moment their financial tier had recalculated, the moment their earnings had dipped below the system's minimum threshold, the decision had already been made for them. Capitalschism-owned housing was the final stage for workers who had slipped beyond self-sufficiency but were still useful enough to extract value from. A worker who could still stand, who could still move, who could still check in for shifts, was worth maintaining, so long as they remained productive.

The relocation was not optional. The notification had made that clear. *Noncompliance will result in deactivation of your work account.* A polite way of saying: *Refuse, and you will no longer exist.* The system never needed to force anyone. It simply removed options until compliance became the only rational choice.

Ona had not reacted when she read the message. She had only closed her device, exhaled slowly, and started packing. Joras had watched her, waiting for her to say something, to ask what they should do, but she hadn't. There was nothing to discuss. They had been moved like this before. They had fought against it, once. That was before they understood that opposition was simply another variable the system accounted for.

They packed quickly. There wasn't much to take. Their lives had already been reduced to the essentials, and even those were subject to scrutiny. The relocation terms included an inventory audit, anything deemed *nonessential* would be confiscated and reabsorbed into the system. That meant no books, no sentimental objects, no personal furniture. Just uniforms, work tools, and the approved standard-issue belongings.

Miklas clutched his stuffed animal, one of the few things he still owned that hadn't been lost to one deduction or another. Ona hesitated before tucking it into a bag. Joras knew what she was thinking. If the system flagged it, it would be taken. If Miklas tried to hold onto it, there could be consequences.

Joras crouched beside his son, voice careful. "Buddy, let's keep it in the bag for now, okay? Just while we move."
Miklas nodded, his grip tightening before he let go.

The transport arrived precisely on schedule. It was automated, faceless, efficient. The system had learned that the fewer human interactions involved in displacement, the less opposition there was. There were no landlords to argue with, no caseworkers to appeal to. Just a vehicle, a time slot, and a message confirming the transition. The doors sealed shut behind them with a quiet finality.

Joras sat rigid, his hands clasped in his lap. Ona stared out the reinforced window, watching the city shift around them. The route bypassed the districts still thriving, avoiding the parts of the city where wealth and comfort remained untouched. The contrast was too stark. It was better this way.

The Capitalschism housing complex loomed ahead, a monolith of identical towers stretching toward the sky, their exteriors smooth and featureless. The structures were optimized for density, designed to house as many workers as possible in as little space as necessary. Efficiency over humanity.

As they approached, Joras felt a strange sensation settle over him, not quite fear, not quite resignation. He had read about places like this. Seen the stories, heard the comparisons. *Company towns*, they had called them in the past. Cities where workers were owned as much as they were employed, where wages were circulated back into the same system that paid them, where debt was an unbreakable cycle. The names had changed. The branding was sleeker. But the mechanics were the same.

They disembarked in silence. A uniformed attendant, not a human, just another automated guide, processed their arrival. Their belongings were scanned, their work assignments updated. Their previous debts had been *consolidated* into a new account, structured into payments directly deducted from their future earnings.

Joras clenched his jaw. There would be no escape now. Any job he took, any contract Ona accepted, every shift they worked would feed back into the balance, ensuring they could never fully repay it. The system had done this before. Not just to them, to thousands, millions. A calculation, perfected over generations.

Their assigned unit was on the twelfth floor. The elevator ride was quiet, the air heavy with sterilized efficiency. When the doors opened, they stepped into a corridor indistinguishable from the last. Identical doors, identical lighting, a manufactured uniformity that blurred space and time.

Joras scanned his wrist at the panel beside their door. The lock released with a soft click.

The unit was small. Smaller than the last. The walls were featureless, the furniture minimal. The system had provided the basics, bunk-style sleeping arrangements, a compact hygiene station, a work terminal integrated into the wall. A single window, but the glass was opaque, filtering in light without revealing anything beyond. There was no view.

Miklas climbed onto the lower bunk, testing the mattress. Ona set their bags down without a word.

Joras sat at the work terminal, staring at the blank screen.

A message appeared. *Welcome to your new residence. Work assignments will be updated within 24 hours. Compliance ensures continued eligibility.*

The words had the same tone as every message before it. Neutral. Professional. The language of inevitability.

Joras exhaled slowly.

This was not a home.

It was a containment zone.

And they were never meant to leave.

He pressed his palms into his knees, his breathing slow, controlled. He had always thought there would be a breaking point, a moment when the system pushed too hard, when people would finally resist, when something inside him would snap and demand more than quiet endurance. But now, sitting in a room that had already calculated his worth down to the fraction of an efficiency rating, he understood the truth.

There was no breaking point.

Only a slow erosion, a carefully managed process of grinding people down until they no longer realized they had been reduced to nothing at all.

Ona sat beside him, her hands resting in her lap. She was thinking the same thing. He knew it without asking.

Miklas shifted under the blanket, his small body curling inward, seeking warmth in a space that offered none.

Joras reached for Ona's hand, gripping it tightly.

The system had already calculated their future.

But it had not accounted for what came after desperation.

That thought stayed with him long after Ona had fallen asleep, long after the room had settled into its automated night cycle, long after the soft hum of the air filtration system became the only sound in the space. He lay there, staring at the ceiling, feeling the weight of something he could not yet name pressing against his chest. It was not hope. Not yet. But it was the shadow of something close, something that resisted the equation laid out for him.

The next morning, he left the unit before Ona and Miklas had stirred. He had no shift scheduled yet, his work assignments were still being optimized for his *new classification*, but he needed to move. The walls felt closer than they had the night before, the air thinner.

The corridors of the complex were already alive with movement. Workers moved in steady streams, their faces unreadable, their steps mechanical. There were no conversations, no laughter, no sign of the things that made people feel human. Just a silent march toward tasks dictated by a system that did not recognize them as anything more than moving parts in a larger mechanism.

Joras found himself drawn toward the cafeteria. It was not hunger that pulled him there but curiosity, a need to see the shape of this world in the daylight. The space was vast, efficient, optimized for function. The food was distributed in controlled portions, adjusted in real time based on a worker's history and productivity level. The screens overhead displayed updates with sterile detachment, *Nutritional efficiency: 89%.* The number fluctuated slightly as transactions were processed, a silent algorithm adjusting the balance of intake against projected output.

He hesitated before stepping forward. Maybe it was the realization that this was it, this was the new system, the new routine, the new way his life would be measured. He felt his body resist, his muscles tense with an instinct he couldn't fully name. It wasn't rebellion, not yet. Just awareness.

Someone cleared their throat beside him.

"You waiting for an invitation?"

Joras turned. The man standing next to him was tall, older, his face lined with the kind of exhaustion that came from years, not months, of this kind of life. His uniform was the same as everyone else's, but there was something in the way he carried himself, a stiffness in his posture that suggested he had not always belonged here.

Joras exhaled. "Just… adjusting."

The man let out a dry chuckle. "That's the trick. You don't."

Joras studied him for a moment. "You been here long?"

The man nodded toward an empty table. "Long enough. Sit."

Joras followed, tray in hand, settling across from him as the room continued its quiet, mechanical rhythm.

"They call me Saif," the man said, breaking a piece of standard-issue bread between his fingers. "Before this, I was a structural engineer."

Joras frowned. "You worked for Capitalschism?"

Saif smirked. "Didn't we all? But yeah, not like this. I was part of their urban expansion division. Helped design some of these places, actually. Back when they still needed human oversight." He took a slow bite, chewing thoughtfully. "That was a mistake."

Joras narrowed his eyes. "What happened?"

Saif gestured vaguely to the room around them. "Same thing that always happens. They fed us the same lines at first, *opportunity*, *growth*, *a future in the new world economy*. Then the AI models improved, the automation took over, and suddenly, my *future* became an overhead expense."

Joras swallowed, staring down at his tray. "And now?"

Saif shrugged. "Now I repair the systems I helped build. They don't trust full automation yet, still need people to keep things from breaking completely. But it won't last. Eventually, the system will optimize that, too."

Joras felt something cold settle in his stomach. "Why do you stay?"

Saif chuckled again, but there was no humor in it. "You tell me. Why are *you* here?"

Joras had no answer.

Saif watched him for a moment, then leaned in slightly. "Look, you're new. I get it. You think maybe there's a way to climb out of this, that if you work hard enough, follow the rules, keep your head down, maybe they'll let you move back up." He shook his head. "They won't. You're not here because you failed. You're here because the system *needs* you here. Because this is how it's designed to work."

Joras stared at him, the words hitting deeper than he wanted to admit.

Saif leaned back, finishing his food with methodical efficiency. "I've seen it happen a thousand times. People come in thinking they're just passing through. But once you're here, you don't leave. You just learn to function."

Joras set his fork down. His appetite had vanished.

Saif stood, collecting his tray. "You'll see. Give it time."

He walked away, blending back into the stream of workers, disappearing as efficiently as he had arrived.

Joras sat there for a long time, staring at the screens tracking food consumption, listening to the low hum of the cafeteria, watching the way everyone moved in quiet synchronization.

The realization came slowly, settling into his bones like a sickness.

Saif was right.

This wasn't just a temporary setback.

This was the *end point.*

The final phase of optimization.

And he had no idea how to escape it.

He returned to the unit later than he had planned, his mind heavy with the weight of what he had learned. Ona was sitting at the work terminal, reviewing the latest financial adjustments. She looked up as he entered, and for a brief moment, he saw something in her expression, hope, or maybe just the remnants of it.

"Did you find anything?" she asked.

Joras hesitated. He could tell her what Saif had said. Could tell her that the system had already decided their future, that there was no path forward, only the endless loop of survival. But he couldn't bring himself to say it.

Instead, he sat down beside her, his fingers brushing against hers, a silent reassurance neither of them fully believed.

"We'll figure it out," he said.
Ona nodded.

Neither of them spoke the truth:

There was no way forward.

Only the weight of a system that had already decided their place.

Joras had never known a place could feel so simultaneously crowded and desolate. The housing complex was alive with movement, with the shuffle of feet and the quiet hum of a thousand workers living under the same oppressive conditions, yet there was no sense of community, no real connection between those who shared its walls. It was a structure designed for efficiency, for function, for extraction. It had no room for anything else.

Every aspect of life inside was regulated, measured, and optimized. The corridors were timed to the movement patterns of peak work hours, the common areas monitored for productivity potential, the living spaces designed for rest, but not comfort. Sleep efficiency trackers were embedded in the walls, their subtle glow reminding occupants that even unconscious hours were being logged, assessed, and adjusted. The system expected them to function like a workforce in perfect synchronicity, never falling behind, never disrupting the flow.

Joras had spent days now observing the rhythm of the place, watching as the workers adapted to its demands. No one lingered. No one spoke unless necessary. Even the smallest interactions were transactional, stripped of warmth. The design of the complex discouraged unnecessary movement, staircases tucked away to ensure reliance on automated lifts, hallways that subtly narrowed the further they extended, creating an illusion of motion without freedom. It was a city within a city, cut off from the rest of the world, a holding zone for those who had outlived their economic potential yet were still too valuable to discard entirely.

He had started to recognize faces. Saif, the former engineer, was one of the few who spoke openly, though his words always carried the weight of someone who had already made peace with their captivity. There was Mara, a former teacher, now reduced to data processing, her skills deemed unnecessary beyond the basic cognitive tasks assigned to her shift schedule. There was Deyvi, who had once run his own small logistics company before Capitalschism absorbed it, leaving him as just another cog in the same machinery he had tried to navigate independently. Each of them had been swallowed whole, their pasts reduced to footnotes, their futures carefully calibrated to ensure maximum output with minimal cost.

And then there were the ones Joras never heard speak, the ones who had been in the complex long enough that they had stopped telling their stories, stopped remembering that they had once been anything else. He watched them move through their assigned routines, their faces blank, their postures slumped in a way that had nothing to do with exhaustion and everything to do with resignation. They no longer looked at their surroundings with curiosity or concern. They no longer paused to take in new information. They had become creatures of pure efficiency, absorbing and executing tasks with the mechanical precision of the system that governed them.

Joras listened to their stories, but more importantly, he watched what the system did to them. He saw how their movements became more mechanical over time, how their reactions dulled, how the spark of resistance flickered and dimmed. The system didn't need violence to enforce its control. It had mastered something more effective, predictability. It made sure that every action led to an expected outcome, that every attempt to push back resulted in an immediate correction, that every worker understood, on a deep and unspoken level, that their fate had already been determined. The system had perfected learned helplessness, training people not just to obey but to cease imagining any other possibility.

The cafeteria was a prime example of this. The food was free, but only within a predefined limit, an amount carefully measured to sustain function but never indulgence. The nutritional efficiency score fluctuated daily, a quiet reminder that even biological needs were subject to optimization. Those who failed to meet their work quotas found their portions subtly reduced, not enough to cause starvation, but enough to reinforce compliance. A worker who performed well might receive a slight increase, a temporary reward that created just enough incentive to maintain effort without ever granting true security. It was an old trick, one that had been used in prisons, in company towns, in factory dormitories throughout history. A worker who believed they could earn their way to safety would push themselves harder than one who had already accepted that they were disposable.

Joras had seen the reports before, how, in the early 20th century, industries had built towns to house their workers, controlling every aspect of their lives, from rent to groceries to healthcare. Wages were paid in company credits, and those credits could only be spent within the system, ensuring that no matter how hard someone worked, they could never truly leave. The modern version was no different. There were no company credits here, only the illusion of choice. Workers were still paid in real currency, but the costs of their existence, rent, food, healthcare, transportation, were all owned by the same system that paid them. Every paycheck was designed to flow directly back into the machine that issued it.

He had asked Saif once if anyone had ever managed to break free, if anyone had saved enough, planned well enough, worked the system just right. Saif had just shaken his head.
"You don't save here," he had said. "You circulate."

The realization had settled into Joras like a sickness.

Even the illusion of personal finance was a joke. The work contracts, the deductions, the incremental debt adjustments, all of it was engineered to maintain equilibrium. No one would ever go bankrupt, not in a way that would make them completely useless to the system, but no one would ever climb out, either. If a worker began to accumulate too much in savings, the system adjusted their expenses. If someone fell too deep into debt, they were offered assistance programs, loans with just enough flexibility to keep them solvent, never enough to grant real freedom. The system could not allow complete destitution. But it also could not allow independence. It needed workers to remain in the delicate balance of survival, never falling so far that they ceased to be useful, never rising so high that they could afford to leave.

Ona had started seeing it, too. She had taken to watching the financial statements, the balance sheets, tracking how their expenses fluctuated in ways that had nothing to do with their actual consumption. The rent adjustments, the automated tax recalibrations, the service fees that appeared and disappeared without explanation.

"They know exactly how much we need to stay alive," she had said one night, staring at the screen. "And they take everything else."

Joras hadn't responded. There was nothing to say.

Miklas had adapted in his own way. He didn't ask for things anymore. Not shoes, not toys, not even extra food. He had learned, in that quiet and terrifying way that children did, that resources were measured, that every request had a cost. He had stopped complaining when he was hungry, had stopped asking when they would leave this place, had stopped expecting the kind of warmth and security that should have been his right. He had learned to pretend he wasn't cold. He had learned to ration his own portions without being told. He had learned, instinctively, to weigh whether his needs were important enough to bring up.

That was the part that broke Joras the most.

He had known, rationally, that this was happening, that the world they lived in had been designed to function this way. But knowing something in theory and watching it play out in real time were two different things. He had spent so long believing that if he just worked harder, if he just kept pushing forward, if he just endured long enough, he could give Miklas something better.

Now, he understood the truth.

This was not a temporary hardship. This was not a rough patch that they would one day escape. This was the system working exactly as it had been designed to.

They were not failing.

They were simply being used.

And deep down, Joras knew, if something didn't change, if they didn't find a way out, if they didn't disrupt the equation that had already been written for them, Miklas would grow up the same way. He would become another name on a work roster, another efficiency rating in the database, another exhausted body in the endless cycle of extraction.

That thought kept Joras awake at night.

That, more than anything, made him wonder if there was still a way to break free.

Ona had started looking, in the quiet moments when she thought he wasn't watching. She was searching for something, a gap in the system, an opportunity, a crack in the foundation. She hadn't said anything yet, but Joras could see it in the way she lingered over certain reports, the way she bookmarked encrypted forums, the way she studied the old protest movements, the failed uprisings, the whispered stories of those who had tried before.

She hadn't given up.

And because of that, Joras couldn't, either.

For now, they moved through the motions. They played their roles. They survived.

But survival was not enough.

Not anymore.

6
Exploitation's New Face

Ona had learned early on that the system did not see her. Not fully. It registered her existence in numbers, in data points, in performance metrics that fluctuated according to some invisible algorithm, but it never saw her as a person. It did not acknowledge exhaustion. It did not recognize fear. It had no function for dignity. It cared only for efficiency, for compliance, for extraction.

Her job had changed since the move. The system had reassigned her based on the latest workforce analysis, matching her to a role that best suited the needs of the complex. The work itself was meaningless, repetitive data validation, error correction for automated logs, small administrative tasks that had been deemed too trivial for full automation but still necessary for the smooth operation of the machine. She was, in essence, a failsafe, a buffer for system imperfections, a human mechanism designed to ensure that the more valuable automation processes continued without interruption.

Her workspace was a row of terminals in a windowless room, filled with other workers who performed identical tasks. There was no conversation. The system discouraged it by tracking their keystrokes, monitoring idle time, flagging deviations. Each workstation was equipped with an efficiency indicator, a visual reminder that their worth was being calculated in real time. A worker who fell below the expected output would be flagged. A worker who exceeded expectations would be offered additional tasks. There were no rewards, only the opportunity to maintain one's position for another day.

And then there were the supervisors.

Officially, the complex did not have human supervisors. The system handled oversight, performance tracking, disciplinary actions. But there were still enforcers, men who had been given authority, not because they were the best workers, but because they were the most willing to act as the system's hands. They were the ones who doled out warnings, who handled disputes, who decided which workers received the most grueling assignments and which ones were granted minor leniencies. They were not leaders. They were just men who had learned to climb within the narrow space the system allowed, men who had accepted that power in this world was not measured by freedom but by the ability to control those with even less.

Ona noticed them immediately.

She had worked enough jobs, had been in enough precarious situations, to recognize the way they moved, the way they watched. There was no outright threat, no explicit danger, but she could feel it in the way they lingered too close, in the way their eyes scanned the rows of workers as if sorting them into categories only they understood. She had seen it before, in the way power operated in places where no one had any real recourse.

It was not long before one of them singled her out.

His name was Callen. He was one of the longer-serving workers, a man who had been in the complex long enough to learn how to bend the rules just enough to get what he wanted. He was not large, not particularly intimidating, but he had a presence, a kind of arrogance that came from knowing that no one would stop him. He was a man who understood how power functioned in a world without oversight, who had learned that authority was not about force but about leverage.

The first time he spoke to her, it was casual. A comment about her work speed, a suggestion that she should slow down, that she was making the rest of them look bad. It was the kind of remark that could have been harmless, but Ona had spent too many years navigating these spaces not to recognize the subtext.

The next time, he made a joke at her expense, something crude but disguised as humor, something that would allow him to claim innocence if she reacted. She ignored him.

That was when he started making it harder for her to ignore him.

He would stand behind her station, watching as she worked, his presence an unspoken challenge. He would make comments just quiet enough that the system's audio monitors wouldn't flag them. He would "correct" her work unnecessarily, forcing her to redo tasks she had already completed, just to remind her that he could. It was never enough to report. Never enough to document. But it was always enough to make her aware that she was being targeted.

She had seen this before. Had seen how it escalated.

And she knew what happened when women spoke up.

The system had no function for complaints like this. There was no HR department, no worker advocacy board, no appeal process. There was only the algorithm, and the algorithm did not recognize harassment. It did not see power imbalances. It did not acknowledge the ways in which certain workers wielded their positions to exploit others. It only saw numbers, only calculated efficiency. And if a worker became a disruption, if they flagged too many issues, if they became a source of inefficiency rather than production, the system removed them.

Ona understood the rules of this world.

So she did what she had always done.

She adapted.

She moved carefully. She kept her head down. She avoided situations that would give him the opportunity to isolate her. She studied his patterns, learned when he was most likely to linger, when he was most likely to push. She adjusted her work habits, slowed herself down just enough to avoid drawing his attention, but not enough to trigger a performance flag.

But it was exhausting.

She came home every night with her body aching, not just from the monotony of the work but from the tension of knowing that every moment in that room was a calculation, a careful negotiation of survival.

Joras noticed, of course.

He had always been able to read her, even when she didn't speak.

But this was different.

This was something she couldn't tell him.

Because she knew what he would do.

And she knew what the consequences would be.

One night, after an especially long shift, she sat across from him at the small table in their unit, watching as he scrolled through his work logs. His brow was furrowed, his fingers tense against the screen.

"How bad is it?" she asked.

Joras exhaled through his nose, rubbing his forehead. "The deductions are getting worse. They raised the service fees again. Adjusted the maintenance costs." He shook his head. "They don't even try to hide it anymore. They know we'll pay because we don't have a choice."

Ona nodded. She had expected as much. The system had already taken full control of their financial existence. It would squeeze them as much as it could without breaking them entirely.

Joras looked up at her then, his gaze lingering.

"You're tired," he said.

She forced a small smile. "We're all tired."

His jaw tightened. "Is something else going on?"

For a brief moment, she considered telling him. Telling him about Callen. About the way he lingered too long. About the way he spoke to her. About the way she had to spend every shift calculating her every move just to avoid making herself a target.

But she didn't.

Because she knew what would happen.

Joras would get angry.

He would confront Callen.

There would be no fight, no violence, because violence wasn't necessary in a place like this. The system didn't tolerate disruptions. It didn't care about fairness or morality or justice. It only cared about stability.

And if Joras disrupted that stability, even for a moment, he would be removed.

The system didn't fire workers. It just reclassified them. Adjusted their risk assessments. Deprioritized their work assignments. It made them invisible until they stopped existing.

She couldn't let that happen.

So she reached across the table and took his hand.

"I'm okay," she said softly.

Joras held her gaze, searching for the truth beneath her words.

After a moment, he nodded.

But she could see it in his eyes.

He didn't believe her.

And deep down, she knew that this was not something she could keep hiding forever.

Joras had always understood the nature of power. It had never been about force alone. Power was in the quiet calculations of those who understood how to manipulate systems, how to turn desperation into obedience, how to make opposition seem not only futile but irrational. Power did not need to shout. It only needed to structure the world in such a way that people convinced themselves that their suffering was normal, that their limitations were self-imposed, that the ceiling above them was natural rather than constructed.

He had spent years learning this lesson, but it was different when it was Ona. Different when it was her coming home exhausted in a way that went beyond physical fatigue. Different when it was her voice, quieter than usual, her movements slightly more measured, her focus split between whatever she was doing and some internal calculation he couldn't yet understand. She wasn't telling him something, and that was what unsettled him the most. Not just that something was wrong, but that she had decided he couldn't know about it.

He didn't ask right away. He had spent enough time navigating the tightrope of their lives to know that confrontation wasn't always the best approach. Instead, he watched. He noted the way she hesitated before leaving for her shift, the way she lingered just a fraction of a second longer at their door. He saw how her shoulders tensed when a new message arrived on her device, how she dismissed certain notifications a little too quickly. He saw the way she avoided discussing anything beyond logistics, keeping their conversations strictly within the realm of necessity, how much they owed, what shifts were available, what they could cut from their already bare budget. She was managing something, carrying something alone.

It wasn't until he overheard two workers talking in the cafeteria that he began to piece it together.

"She'll learn," one of them muttered, barely audible over the low hum of conversation.

Joras had been passing by, half-listening, not intending to stop until he caught the reply.

"They all do," the second worker said. "Or they leave."
The conversation moved on before Joras could hear more, but the weight of those words settled into him like a slow-building pressure. It wasn't a warning. It was a statement of fact. A simple, undeniable truth about how things worked here.

That night, as Ona sat at their work terminal, scrolling through reports with a detached focus, Joras stood in the small space of their unit, hands clenched at his sides.

"What's happening at your job?" he asked.

Ona's fingers hesitated just slightly before she swiped to the next screen.

"Nothing," she said, too evenly.

Joras didn't move. "You don't have to do that," he said. "I know something's wrong."

She sighed, tilting her head back for a moment before looking at him. The expression in her eyes wasn't anger. It wasn't even frustration. It was exhaustion, layered over something else.

"You can't fix this, Joras."

He clenched his jaw. "Tell me anyway."

For a long time, she didn't answer. She just sat there, fingers motionless on the terminal, staring at the data as if it might offer her a way out. Finally, she exhaled, closing her device.

"There's a worker at my job. Callen."

She didn't have to say the rest.

Joras had seen enough of the world to know exactly what she meant.

His breath came slow, controlled. Not because he wasn't angry, but because anger was dangerous here. Because he knew how quickly it could turn into something the system would punish them for.

"What has he done?" he asked, voice steady.

Ona rubbed her temples. "Nothing I can report. Nothing that would register."

That was the problem, wasn't it? The system only acknowledged disruption if it interfered with function. But this kind of power play wasn't meant to disrupt. It was meant to remind people like Ona that they were vulnerable, that they existed at the mercy of those who had even the smallest degree of authority. Callen didn't need to act overtly. He only needed to remind her, again and again, that there was nothing she could do. That was enough.

Joras sat down across from her.

"Does he touch you?"

"No." The answer was immediate, firm. "He's careful."

"Does he threaten you?"

"Not in words."

Joras exhaled sharply. It was exactly what he had feared. Not direct enough to be punished, not obvious enough to be flagged, but unmistakable to those who understood what was happening. It was a game of attrition, a battle not of force but of pressure.

Ona studied him. "Joras, you can't go after him."

He didn't answer.
"I mean it," she said, voice firmer. "If you get flagged, they'll find a reason to remove you. And then what?"

He knew she was right. But knowing did not make it easier.

Instead, he leaned forward, resting his arms on the table. "What do you want to do?"

Ona hesitated. "I don't know."

And that was the worst part. There was no solution. The system had ensured that.

Joras sat there for a long moment, staring at the wall, at the unremarkable, sterile space that was their home, at the evidence of their dwindling autonomy.

Then, slowly, he reached for her hand.

"You're not alone," he said.

Ona's fingers curled around his, a silent acknowledgment.

For now, that was all they had. But Joras knew one thing for certain.

This system had taken everything from them.

But it had not taken their ability to push back.

Not yet.

Joras had never felt more powerless. The system had stripped him of many things, his independence, his choices, his ability to carve out a future for himself and his family, but this was something different. It was one thing to suffer under a machine designed to extract and discard. It was another thing entirely to watch as it turned its silent, insidious gears against the person he loved, grinding down her spirit in a way that left no marks, no visible wounds, only a slow unraveling that she wasn't allowed to name.

He thought about Callen constantly now, even when he didn't want to. The man was nothing. A middle-tier worker, elevated by the smallest sliver of power, using what little control he had to remind those below him that they could never truly escape the hierarchy. Joras had known men like him before. The ones who mistook proximity to authority for real strength. The ones who learned to manipulate the system rather than fight it, who convinced themselves that their ability to exert dominance over someone else made them something more than cogs in the same brutal machine.

The worst part was knowing that Callen would never face consequences. The system didn't acknowledge the kind of exploitation that couldn't be logged in an efficiency report. It didn't recognize what it didn't measure, and it didn't measure anything that didn't directly interfere with productivity. That was how power worked here, it lived in the gaps, in the spaces between oversight and control, in the unspoken understanding that no one would help them.

And yet, despite everything, Ona continued to go to work.

She left in the mornings with the same quiet determination, her posture unwavering, her pace steady. She still came home at the same time, still sat at the table with Miklas, still checked their financial statements with meticulous care. She did not speak of Callen again, not directly, and Joras knew why. This was her battle, and she had already calculated the risks of bringing him into it.

But Joras couldn't let it go.

He tried not to press her, but he paid attention. He noted the shifts in her energy, the tension in her shoulders when she returned home. He watched for changes in her sleep patterns, for the way she hesitated before logging into her work reports, for the small but telling signs that the pressure was getting worse. Ona had always been steady, unshakable even when everything around them collapsed. But now, something was different. Her resilience was still there, but it had become quieter, more brittle, as if she were bracing for something inevitable.

And then one night, she came home later than usual.

Joras had been pacing the small space of their unit, pretending to work, pretending not to notice the time. But when the door finally slid open and she stepped inside, something in her expression made his breath catch.

She was composed. Too composed.

He set down his device. "What happened?"

Ona shook her head, dropping her work bag by the door. "Nothing."

He didn't move. "Ona."

She exhaled slowly, rubbing her temples. "He escalated."

Joras clenched his jaw, his muscles tightening. "How?"

Ona didn't answer right away. She crossed the room, sitting down at the small table, hands folded in front of her. When she finally spoke, her voice was calm, measured.

"He found an excuse to keep me late. Said there was a system issue that needed oversight. It wasn't true, of course. He just wanted me there alone."

Joras sat down across from her, his hands gripping the edges of the table. "And?"

Ona met his gaze. "And I left. But not before he made it clear that this won't stop unless I cooperate."

The words settled in the air between them, heavy and sharp.

Joras inhaled slowly. He had never been a violent man, not by nature, but something inside him burned with the need to act, to retaliate, to do something other than sit here and accept what was happening. But he also knew the truth. He knew that if he went after Callen, it wouldn't be Callen who suffered. It would be them.

Ona watched him carefully. "Joras. You have to promise me something."

He swallowed hard. "What?"

"You can't do anything. Not yet."

His fingers tightened against the table. "Not yet?"

Ona nodded. "I've been thinking."

Joras frowned. "About what?"

She hesitated. "Leaving."

The word was a shock, even though he had known, deep down, that it had been coming.

"Leaving," he repeated.

Ona exhaled. "Not running. Not disappearing. That's not possible. But there are places outside the complex, outside the strictest levels of control. Black zones, unmonitored sectors. If we can get there, we might have a chance."

Joras ran a hand over his face, trying to process what she was saying. "That's not escape, Ona. That's just… another version of this."

She shook her head. "No. It's different. The system doesn't regulate them the same way. It's where people go when they fall off the grid. It's dangerous, but it's better than this."

Joras sat back, his mind racing. He had always imagined that if they left, it would be for something better, something permanent. But this wasn't escape in the way he had once hoped for. It was just another shift in strategy, another way of surviving.

And yet, what was the alternative?

If they stayed, Ona would be at Callen's mercy. Maybe not today, maybe not even next week, but eventually, the system would wear her down the same way it had worn down so many others. Eventually, she would be forced to choose between compliance and erasure. He had seen it before. A worker who refused to conform would find their shifts reassigned to impossible hours, their work ratings mysteriously dropping, their housing eligibility suddenly under review. The system wouldn't need to punish her directly. It would only need to tighten its grip until there was nowhere left to turn.

Ona studied him. "I don't expect you to say yes right now. But I need you to think about it."

Joras nodded slowly.

For the first time in weeks, he felt something other than exhaustion.

He felt possibility.

It wasn't freedom. Not yet.

But it was something close.

And as he looked at Ona, at the quiet determination in her eyes, at the steady resolve beneath her fatigue, he realized something else.

She had already made her decision.

Now, it was only a matter of when.

7
Collective Sparks

Joras had always assumed that opposition was impossible. The system had perfected its methods of control, tightening its grip not with brute force, but with algorithms, efficiency ratings, and the slow erosion of individual agency. It did not need to send enforcers to break the will of its workers. It simply engineered their exhaustion, shaped their desperation, and ensured that every decision was dictated by the relentless calculus of survival.

But as he moved through the complex in the weeks following Ona's revelation, something began to shift in his perception. It wasn't that the system had cracks, he had long suspected that, but rather, that some people had learned how to move within them. It was subtle, almost imperceptible at first. A worker lingering a few seconds longer in a corridor than the efficiency tracking would normally allow. A whispered exchange in the food line that was too quick, too deliberate to be idle conversation. A meeting request on his work terminal that disappeared before he could register the name attached to it.

He wasn't the only one watching. Others were watching him, too.

It started with Saif.

One evening, Joras found himself beside the older man in the communal space, a rare moment of downtime between shifts. The complex was never silent, but at this hour, there was an illusion of stillness, a slowing of movement as workers retreated to their assigned spaces for the few allotted hours of sleep. Saif sat with his usual measured ease, his expression unreadable as he scanned a work report that Joras knew was probably meaningless. The reports were always meaningless. They told workers what they already knew, that they were barely keeping up, that they needed to do more, that their futures had already been written for them.

"Long day?" Saif asked, not looking up.

Joras exhaled. "They all are."

Saif nodded, tapping at his screen idly before setting it aside. He studied Joras then, his gaze sharp, assessing.

"You're thinking about something," he said.

Joras hesitated. He didn't know why, but he felt as if Saif already knew what he was going to say.

"There's no way out of this, is there?" Joras asked finally.

Saif's mouth quirked into something that wasn't quite a smile. "Not in the way you're hoping."

Joras frowned. "What does that mean?"

Saif leaned forward slightly, lowering his voice. "It means that if you're waiting for the system to fail, for some grand collapse that will open the gates and set us free, you'll die waiting. That's not how this works."

Joras felt a cold weight settle in his chest. "Then how does it work?"

Saif was silent for a moment. When he spoke, his voice was even. "The system doesn't break all at once. It erodes. From the inside."

Joras narrowed his eyes. "You sound like someone who knows more than they should."

Saif met his gaze without flinching. "I know enough."

A pause. A calculation. A choice.

Joras swallowed. "If there's something I should know, tell me."

Saif studied him a moment longer before nodding slightly, as if coming to a decision. He reached into his pocket, pulling out a small data chip, placing it between them on the table.

"Take this," he said.

Joras eyed it warily. "What is it?"

"An introduction," Saif said simply.

Joras hesitated before reaching for the chip, his fingers closing around the smooth plastic. It was smaller than he had expected, lighter, but it carried a weight that had nothing to do with its physical mass.

Saif leaned back. "You didn't get it from me."

Joras exhaled slowly, nodding. "Understood."

He left the conversation with more questions than answers, but he knew one thing with certainty, he had just stepped into something much larger than himself.

That night, when Ona asked if everything was okay, he almost told her. Almost.
But he didn't. Not yet.

Instead, he lay awake long after she had fallen asleep, turning the chip over in his fingers, feeling the shape of the choice before him.

The next day, when he plugged the chip into his work terminal, it didn't behave like standard data storage. There was no immediate file, no visible log entry. Instead, a simple message appeared on the screen, words typed in a stark, unadorned font.

Sublevel 3. Maintenance corridor. 22:00.

Joras stared at it for a long moment before the message vanished. The terminal reset itself, returning to its normal interface as if nothing had happened.

For a long time, he did nothing. He continued his shift, followed his assigned routes, completed his deliveries with the same automated precision as always. But the message remained in his mind, like a quiet pressure against his thoughts.

He wasn't sure what he expected when he arrived at the maintenance corridor later that night. He had moved carefully, taking indirect routes, ensuring that his presence there would seem incidental if anyone happened to be watching. The corridor itself was dimly lit, the overhead lamps casting long shadows along the concrete walls.

There was no one there.

He waited. Five minutes. Ten.

Then, just as he was about to turn back, a door at the far end of the corridor clicked open. A figure stepped out.

A woman.

She was tall, with sharp features and a gaze that held none of the passive resignation Joras had grown accustomed to seeing in the complex. She regarded him for a moment before tilting her head slightly.

"You're the new one." It wasn't a question.

Joras hesitated. "I—"

"You came because of Saif."

Again, not a question.

Joras nodded.

The woman exhaled, then gestured for him to follow.

She led him through a narrow passageway, deeper into the maintenance sector, until they reached what appeared to be an old service room. Inside, the lighting was low, the walls lined with outdated equipment and storage racks. But it wasn't empty.

There were others.

Joras counted at least seven people, each seated around a makeshift table, their faces alert, wary. They studied him as he entered, measuring, evaluating.

The woman motioned for him to sit.

"I'm Lian," she said, leaning against the wall. "I assume you have questions."
Joras swallowed. "A few."

Lian smirked. "That's good. Means you're not an idiot."

A man at the table chuckled. "Well, he's here, so we'll see."

Joras exhaled. "What is this?"

Lian's expression turned serious. "This is the part of the city the system pretends doesn't exist."

Joras frowned. "That doesn't answer my question."

Lian nodded, conceding the point. "We're workers. Just like you. Just like everyone in this place. But we're also something else."

Joras waited.

"We are the ones who refuse to be optimized," Lian said finally. "We are the ones who remember what it means to be free."

Joras's breath hitched slightly. The words felt reckless. Dangerous. And yet, he didn't look away.

“You think this is possible?” he asked. “Beating the system?”

Lian smiled, but there was no amusement in it. “Beating it? No. Not all at once. But resistance doesn’t have to mean toppling everything overnight.”

Joras frowned. “Then what does it mean?”

Lian leaned forward.

“It means making them bleed,” she said. “It means finding the cracks. It means teaching people to see the cage around them. It means reminding the system that we are not just numbers in a ledger.”

Joras felt his pulse quicken.

For the first time in a long time, he felt something unfamiliar.

It wasn’t resignation.

It wasn’t even fear.

It was possibility.

And for the first time, he let himself believe that maybe, just maybe, there was still something worth fighting for.

Joras left the meeting with a strange weight in his chest, something that felt like a collision of fear and hope, two opposing forces grinding against each other like tectonic plates beneath the surface of his mind. The words they had spoken echoed in his thoughts long after he had returned to his unit, long after he had settled into the familiar rhythm of his work the next morning. He had spent years believing that the system was an immovable force, a monolith against which opposition was not only impossible but irrational. And yet, here were people who refused to accept that truth, people who had found ways to move within the cracks, to push back, to carve out spaces where they could still act with intent rather than mere compliance.

He told himself he needed time to process, to consider, to weigh the risks. But the truth was, he had already decided. He had decided the moment he stepped into that maintenance room, the moment he looked around and saw faces that had not yet been fully beaten into submission. He had decided the moment Lian spoke, her voice carrying the certainty of someone who understood exactly what was at stake.

Still, he did not speak of it to Ona. Not yet.

Not because he didn't trust her, but because he knew that she would see the risk with sharper clarity than he did. Ona did not allow herself to chase possibility unless she had first dissected every consequence. It was not pessimism, it was survival. She would ask questions he wasn't ready to answer. She would demand a certainty he could not yet offer. And more than anything, he did not want to place this weight on her shoulders. She was already carrying too much.

So he waited.

He continued his shifts, moving through the motions with the same outward detachment, but inside, he was watching, learning, searching for the patterns that had been invisible to him before. And slowly, the shape of the underground movement began to emerge.

It was not an organization in the way he had once imagined. There were no clear leaders, no hierarchies, no manifestos. It was something looser, more fluid, a network of individuals who understood that resistance could not be structured in the same way as the system they opposed. It had to be adaptable, decentralized, built on trust rather than authority. Information passed in coded messages hidden in work logs, in seemingly casual conversations held just outside the range of surveillance, in digital spaces designed to disappear the moment they were accessed.

Most of what they did was small, almost imperceptible at first glance. A supply shipment delayed by a misfiled work order. A maintenance log subtly altered to misdirect an automated repair. Data records that shifted just enough to introduce errors into the system's predictive models. It was not about immediate sabotage, it was about making the machine falter, making it doubt itself, forcing it to expend resources correcting mistakes that should not exist. The system functioned on the principle of total control, on the belief that it could anticipate every variable, every behavior, every outcome. If enough of those calculations proved incorrect, if enough unpredictability was introduced, the entire structure would begin to wobble.

Joras found himself drawn into these small acts of defiance with a cautious but growing sense of purpose. At first, he followed instructions blindly, trusting that those who had been doing this longer knew what they were doing. But as he learned, as he began to see the interlocking gears of the machine in a way he never had before, he started to think beyond the tasks he was given. He started to notice new vulnerabilities, gaps in the system's oversight that could be exploited.

And yet, the fear remained.

Not fear for himself, he had long since accepted that his own existence was expendable to the machine. It was the fear for Ona, for Miklas, for what would happen if he miscalculated. The system did not punish dissent immediately. It was patient, methodical. It would not make a martyr of him, it would simply begin to tighten the invisible noose, shifting the conditions of his life so subtly that by the time he realized what was happening, it would already be too late.

He saw it happen to others.

A man named Rami, who had worked in logistics, disappeared from the shift roster overnight. No explanation. No warning. His unit was reassigned within hours, his belongings removed as if he had never existed. Someone muttered that he had gotten sloppy, that he had triggered one of the system's deeper security sweeps. Lian said nothing. Neither did anyone else.

Joras understood the message.

The system was watching. Always. And yet, he did not step back.

Instead, he found himself sinking deeper, the weight of the risk balanced against the quiet, insistent pull of something he had not allowed himself to feel in a long time.

Hope.

Not the naïve, childish kind that believed in sweeping revolutions, in sudden transformations, in the toppling of structures overnight. No, this was something different. This was the kind of hope that understood the scale of the fight, that recognized the impossibility of immediate victory but refused to surrender anyway. It was the hope of erosion, of slow, deliberate dismantling, of planting cracks that would one day split the foundation apart.

But hope, he knew, was dangerous.

And eventually, Ona would notice.

It was inevitable.

And when she did, he would have to answer for it.

It happened one evening, just as he had feared.

He had been careful, or so he had thought. He had taken the longer routes home, varied his patterns, ensured that he never appeared to be deviating from the expected parameters of his routine. But Ona knew him too well. She had spent too many years reading the quiet shifts in his expression, the subtle differences in his posture, the slight hesitations in his voice.

"You're doing something," she said.

Joras didn't look up from his work terminal. "I don't know what you mean."

Ona set her device down, folding her arms. "Don't do that. Don't act like I can't see it."

Joras exhaled, rubbing a hand over his face. "Ona—"

"You're not as tired," she interrupted. "Not in the same way. You come home late, but you don't look like you've been crushed into the floor anymore. You look..." She hesitated. "Like you're planning something."

Joras closed his eyes. He should have known better than to think she wouldn't see it.

He took a slow breath. "I found something," he admitted.

Ona's jaw tightened. "Something, or someone?"

Joras met her gaze. "Both."

She didn't speak right away. Instead, she studied him, her expression unreadable. When she finally did speak, her voice was quiet.

"Tell me everything."

And so he did.

He told her about Saif. About the meeting in the maintenance corridor. About Lian, about the others, about the way they were working to disrupt the system from within. He told her about the risks, the disappearances, the possibility that every step he took was being watched.

When he finished, she was silent for a long time.

Then she leaned forward.

"Do you trust them?"

Joras hesitated. "I trust what they're trying to do."

Ona exhaled, her fingers pressing into the edge of the table. "Then we have to be smarter than them."

Joras frowned. "What do you mean?"

Ona met his gaze, her expression sharp, calculated.

"I mean that resistance is only half the battle," she said. "The other half is knowing when to walk away before the system catches up."

Joras studied her, realization dawning. She wasn't telling him to stop. She was telling him to be careful.

She was telling him to fight, but to fight like someone who intended to survive.

For the first time in a long time, Joras felt something shift between them. Not distance. Not tension. But something closer to understanding.

And in that moment, he knew.

They weren't just trying to survive anymore. They were preparing for something more.

Joras had expected hesitation from Ona. Had expected fear, resistance, a warning to step back before they lost everything. But instead, she had done something far more unsettling, she had adapted. She had listened, absorbed the information, and immediately begun thinking in terms of strategy. Not whether they should continue, but how they could continue and remain one step ahead of the system. It was the same way she approached every problem, with the ruthless efficiency of someone who had learned long ago that survival depended on calculation rather than impulse.

And yet, even as she spoke, even as she mapped out contingencies and countermeasures, he saw something else flickering beneath the surface. Something deeper than exhaustion.

Rage.

It was not the loud, burning kind, not the reckless fire that made men like Callen dangerous. It was cold, deliberate, coiled like a steel wire beneath her composure. The kind of rage that did not explode but endured. The kind that did not demand retribution in the moment but instead committed every injury to memory, filed it away, prepared to unleash it at the precise moment when it would matter most.

Joras had always admired her mind, her ability to see paths he had not yet considered. But now, watching her, he realized something else. Ona had been waiting for this.

For an opportunity.

For an opening.

For the moment when all the injustices she had endured, all the ways the system had shaped and confined her, could finally be used against it.

He had thought he was the one stepping into something larger than himself. But perhaps Ona had always known they would reach this point. Perhaps she had only been waiting for him to catch up.

Days passed, and Joras continued his work with the underground movement, but now, he was not alone. Ona did not attend meetings, did not put herself on the same front lines, but she did something just as critical, she began to gather information.

She was careful, methodical, never asking questions outright, never drawing attention to herself. Instead, she listened. She observed. She watched the patterns of the system in a way that Joras had never considered, analyzing how work assignments were distributed, how efficiency ratings fluctuated, how certain workers were quietly shifted from one department to another before disappearing entirely. She noted which corridors had blind spots in surveillance coverage, which access points were still reliant on human oversight rather than automation.

She wasn't just surviving anymore.

She was mapping the prison from the inside.

And the more she learned, the clearer it became, the system was not invulnerable.

It was powerful, yes. Omnipresent, overwhelming, structured to prevent opposition before it could begin. But it was still built by people. And people made mistakes.

One of those mistakes was the assumption of absolute compliance.

The system believed that once a worker had been broken, they would stay broken. That once they had accepted their place, they would not look for ways to disrupt it. It did not account for what happened when people reached the point beyond fear.

Joras felt it shifting, not just in himself, not just in Ona, but in others. The quiet anger beneath every exhausted conversation. The stolen moments where workers exchanged glances that carried more weight than words.

The unspoken acknowledgment that they all knew they were being crushed. And that, maybe, just maybe, they didn't have to accept it.

One night, Lian approached Joras after a meeting, her expression unreadable.

"You're moving differently," she said.

Joras hesitated. "What do you mean?"

Lian studied him for a long moment before smirking. "You're thinking beyond survival now."

Joras exhaled. "Shouldn't I be?"

Lian tilted her head slightly. "Most people don't. They get caught up in the resistance itself, in the fight. They forget to ask the bigger question."

Joras frowned. "Which is?"

Lian's gaze sharpened. "What comes after?"
Joras felt something tighten in his chest. He had been so focused on pushing back, on creating instability, that he hadn't considered what they were building toward. Did they have an end goal, or were they simply trying to make the system hurt?

He thought about Ona. About the way she had begun collecting information, the way she had shifted from simply enduring to actively dismantling the illusion of inevitability.

And he realized that she had already started answering Lian's question.

Not just how to fight.

But how to win.

They were sitting at their table that night, Ona scrolling through work reports, Joras pretending to review his own, when she spoke without looking up.

"There's a recall request on the sanitation automation."

Joras blinked. "What?"

She tapped something on her screen, tilting it slightly so he could see. "One of the maintenance bots failed its last three diagnostic cycles. They're requisitioning human workers to inspect the whole system manually."

Joras frowned. "And?"

Ona finally looked at him. "The sanitation system is connected to the central logistics hub."

Joras stared at her, the pieces clicking together in his mind.

The sanitation system was critical to the complex's operations, ensuring waste was removed, recycled, repurposed. It was rarely accessed directly by human workers, but if a manual inspection had been requested…

It meant entry points that were usually off-limits would be temporarily accessible.

Joras exhaled. "How long do we have?"
"Two days before the request is processed. After that, the system will reroute tasks, and the window closes."

Joras set down his device, his mind racing. "If we can get into the logistics hub…"

Ona nodded. "We can disrupt supply tracking. Delivery schedules. Even financial records."

Joras rubbed a hand over his face. "That's not just small sabotage, Ona. That's real damage."

She met his gaze, her expression unwavering. "I know."

Joras swallowed. He had spent weeks, months, believing that hope was something fragile, something that had to be held carefully, nurtured, kept alive with quiet defiance. But this, this was not fragile. This was calculated. This was intentional.

And for the first time, he saw the full extent of what Ona had been planning. Not escape. Not just survival. A collapse. A deliberate, methodical collapse of the very system that had been designed to keep them docile.

Joras exhaled, leaning forward, lowering his voice. "How do we do it?"

Ona's eyes darkened with something that looked almost like certainty.

"I already have a plan."

The next night, they went to Lian.

Joras explained. Ona filled in the details.

Lian listened, her expression unreadable, her arms crossed, her mind clearly running through every angle. When they finished, she was silent for a long moment.

Then, slowly, she nodded.

"You two are either the smartest people I've met," she said, "or the most reckless."
Joras smirked. "Maybe both."

Lian exhaled, rubbing her temples. "This is bigger than anything we've done before."

"I know," Ona said.

"If we fail—"

"We won't," Ona interrupted.

Lian raised an eyebrow. "You sound sure."
Ona's gaze was steady. "I am."

Lian studied her, then glanced at Joras.

"Alright," she said finally. "Let's burn this place down."

Joras felt something cold and electric surge through him.

For the first time in his life, he wasn't just reacting to the system's oppression.

He was moving first.

He looked at Ona, and in her eyes, he saw what he had always known but never fully understood.

She had never been broken.

She had been waiting.

And now?

Now, the system was going to pay for everything it had taken.

8
The Protest Algorithm

Joras had never imagined himself as part of something like this. Resistance, in his mind, had always belonged to history, to books about revolutions that had already happened, to figures who had risked everything for the vague promise of something better. He had always assumed that change came from somewhere else, from people who had the means to fight, from those who were already on the outside of the machine, pushing against it. Never from those caught inside its gears. Never from people like him.

But now, sitting in a dimly lit maintenance corridor with Lian, Ona, and a handful of others, staring at the outline of their first real coordinated action, he understood something he had never considered before. Resistance was not always a grand event. It did not always begin with a declaration or an uprising or a single moment of defiance that turned the tide of history. Sometimes, it began with something much smaller. A whisper instead of a roar. A single miscalculation in the system's predictive models. A carefully planted disruption in the seamless, automated flow of control.

It began with a protest that the system did not yet realize was a threat.

Lian paced in front of the small group, her movements controlled, her mind clearly running through every possible outcome. The plan had been discussed, refined, pulled apart and put back together a dozen times over the past week. Now, there was no time left for hesitation.

"This has to look spontaneous," she said. "The second the system registers coordination, it'll shut us down before we start. That means no centralized messaging, no single point of origin. We don't launch this from a known network. We let it grow on its own."

Ona nodded, arms crossed. "And we control the narrative before Capitalschism does."

Joras exhaled. He had spent the past several nights analyzing the patterns of algorithmic suppression, mapping the ways in which the system detected and dismantled anything that could be interpreted as dissent. The key was unpredictability. The system thrived on data, on trends, on forecasting human behavior down to its most granular details. But there were gaps. There were places where its models failed, where it had not yet learned to recognize the ways in which people were adapting to its presence.

The plan was to exploit those gaps.

"It starts with something small," Joras said. "Something that doesn't trigger immediate intervention. A minor complaint about working conditions. A delayed wage adjustment. A system error that people already know exists. We seed frustration, not rebellion."

Lian smirked. "And once people start talking?"

"Once they're talking," Ona said, "we guide the conversation without them realizing they're being guided."

That was the brilliance of it. The system could shut down a coordinated movement the moment it was detected, but it could not erase dissatisfaction that appeared organic. It could not intervene in conversations that were framed as minor grievances rather than outright dissent. It could not preemptively silence workers who were simply asking questions about policies that were, on paper, supposed to be fair.

By the time Capitalschism realized what was happening, the conversation would have already spread beyond its control.

Joras studied the others in the room. "This only works if we stay ahead of it. If we push too hard, too fast, we trigger suppression. If we move too slowly, we lose momentum."

Lian cracked her knuckles. "Then we hit them exactly where they're weakest. The perception of stability."

Ona pulled up a screen, displaying a list of key data points, metrics that, to an outside observer, looked innocuous but were, in reality, the foundation of how Capitalschism maintained the illusion of control. Worker satisfaction ratings. Compliance trends. Employee retention statistics. These were the numbers that shareholders and executives relied on to justify their authority. If those numbers shifted too quickly, if discontent became visible in a way that could not be dismissed as an anomaly, then even the most detached decision-makers would be forced to react.

And once they reacted, they would reveal their hand.

"We make them show people what they really are," Ona said. "Before they even realize they're doing it."

Joras exhaled slowly. The logic was sound. If they could manipulate the system into suppressing something too early, too forcefully, before it had reason to do so, then the workers who had previously been indifferent would suddenly see what Joras and the others already knew, his was not a company. This was a prison.

Lian grinned. "Let's light the match."

The first phase was so subtle that even Joras had moments where he questioned whether it would work. It began with carefully placed comments on internal forums, small complaints about shift scheduling and workload distribution. These were things that workers complained about all the time, but this time, responses were strategically planted.

“I heard they’re cutting shift bonuses again.”

“Anyone else notice how overtime pay has been delayed three times this month?”

“The system says my hours are incorrect, but payroll won’t fix it. Happened to anyone else?”

There was no call to action. No direct challenge to authority. Just dissatisfaction, spreading like a low-grade fever through the workforce. And then, once the complaints had circulated enough, they introduced the next layer, speculation.

“The adjustment rates are off this month. If the system is broken, how many of us are getting shorted?”

“Probably a test to see how much they can take before we say something.”

“Does anyone actually know who’s running payroll, or is it just the algorithm now?”

Still no direct rebellion. Still nothing that could be flagged as an organized effort. But now, there was paranoia. The idea that maybe things were not as stable as they seemed. The idea that maybe they were already being played.

And then, when the conversation had reached the right level of anxiety, they introduced the final layer, documentation. Screenshots of discrepancies. Logs of payroll errors. Records of changes to contract terms that had never been announced. Proof, undeniable and unfiltered, that the system was manipulating workers in real-time.

And that was when people started getting angry.

Joras watched it happen in real-time. He saw the shift, the way discussions went from quiet grumbling to open frustration. And he knew that somewhere, behind the layers of algorithms and automated oversight, Capitalschism was watching too.

"They'll move soon," Ona murmured beside him, watching the screen.

Joras nodded. "They have to."

Because now, workers weren't just complaining. They were talking to each other. And that was the one thing the system could not allow.

The suppression began almost immediately.

Forums were locked. Posts were deleted mid-conversation. Workers who had been most vocal suddenly found themselves reassigned to inconvenient shifts, their schedules rearranged to prevent further discussion. It was a textbook response, one the system had used a thousand times before. Disrupt the lines of communication. Make dissenters invisible. Introduce just enough fear to discourage further participation.
But this time, it didn't work. Because now, the suppression itself had become proof.
Joras watched as new conversations popped up in encrypted channels, in whispered exchanges during shift transitions.

"They shut down the forum. Why?"

"If there was nothing wrong, why delete the posts?"

"This isn't random. They're doing this on purpose."

And just like that, the protest had already evolved beyond their control. It was no longer a campaign they were orchestrating. It was a reaction that Capitalschism itself had triggered.

Joras exhaled. "We just won the first round."

Ona shook her head. "We've won nothing yet."

She was right. Because now, Capitalschism would stop suppressing quietly. Now, it would escalate.

And for the first time, Joras understood exactly what that meant. This was no longer just about pushing the system. This was a fight.

And he had no idea how far the other side was willing to go. The crackdown came faster than Joras had expected. Within hours, Capitalschism moved beyond quiet algorithmic suppression and into direct intervention. It started with security patrols, visible, deliberate, a show of force meant to remind everyone that the system was watching. Workers who had never drawn attention to themselves before suddenly found their shifts reassigned, their workloads increased. Random efficiency audits became frequent, conveniently targeting those who had engaged in the now-deleted discussions. It was a warning, unspoken but clear.

But the real blow came when they disabled the internal messaging network. Without warning, workers were locked out of private communication channels. The system cited an unexpected software update, a maintenance cycle, a temporary issue that would be resolved soon. But Joras knew better. They all did. This was suppression, plain and simple. The company didn't just want to remove the conversations, it wanted to erase the very possibility of them.

And yet, Capitalschism had made a mistake.

By acting so quickly, by clamping down with such obvious force, it had confirmed what many workers had only suspected before: that there was something worth hiding. If the protests had been nothing, if the complaints had been meaningless, the system would have ignored them. The fact that it reacted with such immediate aggression proved otherwise.

Joras watched as frustration turned to anger. People who had hesitated before were now speaking in hushed voices, exchanging glances filled with something beyond fear. He saw it in the break rooms, in the corridors between shifts, workers who had always kept their heads down were now looking at each other, really looking, as if seeing for the first time that they were not alone in their suffering. The system had relied on isolation, on convincing every individual worker that their struggles were unique, that their hardships were personal failings rather than deliberate design. But now, that illusion was crumbling.

Ona was the first to say what Joras had already been thinking.

"They overplayed their hand."

She sat beside him in their unit, eyes scanning the encrypted chat logs she had managed to pull from the back-end of the system. The official channels were down, but people had found other ways. Workers were sharing external contact details, reviving old, abandoned message boards, rediscovering the kind of underground communication networks that had existed before the system had made them obsolete.

Joras exhaled. "They think they can choke this out before it spreads."

Ona nodded. "They don't realize it's already spread."

That was the thing about fear, it could be used as a tool, but only if people believed they had no other choice. If fear was met with too much pressure, if it was applied too directly, it became something else. It became defiance.

And that was what was happening now.

Joras had spent his life inside systems like this, adjusting to their demands, learning how to survive within the invisible boundaries they placed around him. But now, for the first time, he was watching people test those boundaries, push against them in ways that felt reckless and dangerous but also necessary. It was as if they had been waiting for permission to fight back, waiting for a sign that it was possible, that they weren't the only ones suffocating under the weight of the system's control.

And so, as Capitalschism tightened its grip, the movement did not dissolve. It adapted.

The next phase came naturally, almost effortlessly, as if the resistance had always been there, waiting just beneath the surface. Without internal communication networks, workers turned to external ones. Encrypted channels spread among trusted groups, passed through QR codes hidden in shift logs, disguised as harmless data reports. Messages were encoded in scheduling updates, in shared documents that appeared innocuous but contained instructions buried beneath layers of automated formatting.

And most importantly, they went public.

It started with an anonymous leak. Screenshots of deleted forum posts. Records of payroll inconsistencies. Evidence of wage suppression and manipulation hidden within the automated deduction systems. Someone, Joras still didn't know who, dumped everything onto an external network, an old worker's advocacy site that had long since fallen into disuse but still had enough of a following to gain traction.

Within hours, the leak was spreading beyond the complex.

Ona saw it first. She sat up suddenly, her device screen glowing in the dim light of their unit, her expression unreadable.

"They're talking about it outside."

Joras leaned over, reading the messages flooding the advocacy forums, the social media threads filling with speculation. Workers in other regions were commenting, comparing notes, realizing that the same patterns of suppression were happening to them. The system had always operated under the assumption that workers wouldn't connect the dots, that isolated frustration would remain just that, isolated.

But now, the dots were connecting themselves.

And once that happened, there was no going back.

Lian's voice crackled through the secure channel later that night, her tone carrying something between excitement and exhaustion.

"They're rattled," she said. "They've already started damage control, issuing official statements about worker concerns being taken 'seriously.' They're pretending this is just about payroll discrepancies."

Joras exhaled. "They don't want it to become something bigger."

"They're too late," Ona said.

Lian chuckled. "Yeah. Yeah, I think they are."

But they all knew what was coming next. Capitalschism would not let this spiral any further. The first crackdown had been digital. The next would be physical. And when that happened, there would be no more illusions.

Joras had thought, once, that the system would never resort to open violence, that it had evolved beyond such primitive displays of power. But now, as he watched the growing momentum of their movement, he understood that violence had only ever been reserved for those who could not be controlled in other ways.

And for the first time, the system was afraid. Which meant it was about to show its teeth.

The shift from digital suppression to physical retaliation was inevitable. Joras knew it. They all did. The moment the movement spilled beyond the controlled confines of Capitalschism's internal networks, the moment the outside world took notice, the system had lost the ability to control the narrative entirely through quiet deletions and reassignments. That meant it had to escalate. And when the system escalated, it did not do so with hesitation.

It began with patrols. Not the usual efficiency monitors, not the subtle algorithmic nudges that pushed workers into compliance, but real enforcers, uniformed security personnel who had, up until now, remained in the background, unseen unless a situation absolutely required intervention. Now, they were everywhere. They walked the corridors in pairs, stood at the entrances of work zones, stationed themselves near break areas and housing complexes. They didn't need to say anything. Their presence alone sent the message: We know what you're doing. Stop now.

It was too late for intimidation alone to work. The movement had momentum now, fueled by the very suppression that was supposed to contain it. The workers had seen the system react in real-time, had watched it scramble to shut them down. And in doing so, Capitalschism had confirmed everything they had only suspected before. This wasn't about productivity. It was about control. And that realization, once seen, could not be unseen. Joras felt the change in the air, a charged tension humming beneath the surface of daily operations. Conversations were shorter but heavier, coded with meanings that had not existed before. Workers moved through their shifts with the same mechanical precision, but there was something different in their movements now. A quiet opposition. A refusal to break.

And then, one evening, the inevitable happened.

A worker, someone Joras barely knew, was pulled from his station during shift rotation. It was done quietly, efficiently, with all the practiced ease of a system that had long ago perfected the art of making people disappear. One moment, he was there, scanning inventory updates like everyone else. The next, two security officers were at his side, hands firm on his arms, guiding him out of the work zone.

Except this time, there were questions.

Joras saw it happen from across the room. Saw the flicker of hesitation in the other workers, the way heads turned, the way hands momentarily paused in their automated motions before continuing.

"What did he do?"

A simple question. One that should have been ignored. One that the system, in its usual mode of operation, would have allowed to drift into the air, unanswered.

But the officer made a mistake. He responded.

"Efficiency violation."

That was all he said. Two words. Cold, detached, delivered with the certainty of someone who had never needed to justify their authority before. The shift floor fell silent. The hum of machines, the flickering of status monitors, the distant churn of automated logistics, these things continued, but the workers did not.

For the first time in Joras's memory, they stopped.

Not in unison. Not all at once. But in small, deliberate acts of defiance. A hand lingering on a console instead of swiping to confirm a task. A delay in movement, a hesitation in compliance. The chain reaction spread, subtle at first, but growing, spreading through the work zone like an unseen signal passing between them.

Joras met Ona's gaze from across the room. She had seen it too. This was it. The moment the system had lost control.

And then, the worker being escorted out, his name was Darik, Joras realized distantly, spoke.

"I did everything right."

His voice was steady. Not pleading. Not desperate. Just… true. And that was the moment the dam broke.

Another worker stepped forward. "He's been here longer than half of us. He trained me."

"Wasn't he on the productivity leaderboard last month?"

The questions came fast, overlapping, a rising wave of noise that the system had not prepared for. The officers hesitated, glancing at each other. There had been no protocol for this, no expectation that workers would demand an explanation. The system had built its power on quiet acceptance, on the understanding that people obeyed not because they were forced, but because they had been conditioned to believe there was no alternative.

But now, they were asking why. And that was the most dangerous thing of all. Joras didn't think. He moved.

"Darik stays." His voice was firm, steady, louder than he intended. The words carried across the floor, settling into the silence like a thrown stone in still water.
The officer nearest to him turned sharply. "You don't decide that."

Joras held his ground. "Neither do you."

The officer exhaled sharply, adjusting his stance. He reached for his tablet, likely preparing to flag Joras in the system for noncompliance. But before he could input anything, another voice rang out.

"Darik stays."

Joras turned. It was Lian. She stepped forward from her station, arms crossed, face unreadable but unmistakably resolute.
Then another voice. And another. Until, all at once, the floor was no longer silent.

Joras watched it unfold, barely able to process the shift. This wasn't just a protest anymore. This was refusal. The system could not fire them all. It could not suppress an entire shift team without creating a cascade of disruptions that would ripple through every layer of the operation. If they stood together, if they held the line here, the system would have to retreat. It would have to acknowledge, for the first time, that it did not have complete control.

The officers hesitated. Joras could see them calculating, running through response protocols that had not accounted for this scenario. This was not an isolated act of defiance. This was collective action.

And collective action was something the system feared more than anything.
Then, after what felt like an eternity, the lead officer's tablet chirped with a system update. He glanced down, frowned, then exhaled sharply.

"The reassignment is postponed." His voice was tight with frustration, but Joras heard the truth beneath it.

They had won. For now.

The officers turned, moving briskly toward the exit, Darik left standing, stunned, as the shift floor remained frozen in the aftershock of what had just happened. Joras exhaled, the tension still coiled in his chest, his mind already racing toward what would come next.

Ona reached his side. "This isn't over."

Joras nodded. "No. But it's a start."

And as he looked around at the workers still standing, still watching, still waiting, he realized something else.

This wasn't just the start of a protest.

It was the beginning of a revolution.

9
Betrayal and Sacrifice

Joras had known from the start that the system would not allow their defiance to stand unchallenged. He had prepared himself for the inevitable retaliation, had steeled himself against the fear of what would come. But he had made one fatal mistake. He had assumed that the greatest threat to their movement would come from the outside.

He had not considered betrayal.

The first sign was subtle, almost easy to dismiss as paranoia. A missing transmission, a shift in the timing of security rotations that could have been coincidence. Lian had been the first to notice, her instincts sharpened by years of watching the system's patterns. She had called a meeting, voices hushed, tension thick in the air as they reviewed their last few operations.

"We have a leak," she had said, her voice flat, unreadable. "Someone has been feeding information to Capitalschism."

Joras felt the words settle into his bones like ice. It was not an accusation. It was a certainty.

Ona stiffened beside him, her eyes scanning the faces in the dimly lit space, calculating, already running through the possibilities. The network had been built on trust, on the quiet understanding that they were all fighting for the same thing. But trust was fragile. And the system had ways of finding the cracks.

Lian continued, pulling up a map of recent security sweeps. "They adjusted their response times. This isn't just standard risk mitigation. They knew where we were going to be."

Joras exhaled slowly, pressing his hands against his knees to steady himself. "How much do they know?"

Lian met his gaze. "Enough."

Silence. Ona was the first to break it. "Then we need to act now. Before they move on us." But it was already too late.

They came for Joras two nights later.

The complex had always been watched, but security had never been a visible force, never an overt presence in their daily lives. The system preferred subtlety. It preferred to erase problems rather than confront them directly. But this time, it was different.

He had been moving through the maintenance sector, reviewing the latest recalibrations with Saif, when the alert hit his device.

Mandatory reassignment notice: Immediate enforcement required. Noncompliance will result in termination.

Joras barely had time to process the words before the corridor filled with motion.

The enforcers were not like the usual efficiency monitors. These were not the faceless security patrols that observed from the shadows, waiting for algorithmic permission to intervene. These men were different. Heavily armored, their presence designed not to maintain order, but to impose control.

Joras didn't run. There was nowhere to run to.

Hands seized his arms, the grip firm, impersonal. His device was stripped from him before he could react, his identification processed with ruthless efficiency.

For a moment, he struggled against the restraint, but the response was immediate. A short burst of electrical current seared through his nervous system, dropping him to his knees in a wave of searing pain. Not enough to incapacitate permanently. Just enough to remind him that he was no longer a person. He was a variable being corrected.

Saif stood frozen a few feet away, his expression carefully blank, his hands clenched into fists. There was nothing he could do. Nothing anyone could do.

Joras looked up, forcing his vision to clear. The lead officer, a man whose face was eerily devoid of expression, met his gaze. "You are being reassigned," he said. "You will not resist."

Joras exhaled, steadying his breathing. He turned his head just slightly, enough to see Saif, enough to hope that he could read the unspoken message in his eyes.

Tell Ona. Get her out.

Then they dragged him away.

Ona knew something was wrong the moment her device failed to sync. The delay was minor, imperceptible to anyone who wasn't watching for it, but she had trained herself to see patterns in the system's behavior. A lag in network response meant recalibration. Recalibration meant a purge.
And purges meant someone had already been taken.

She felt the ice settle in her stomach before the confirmation came. Saif's message was short, coded, barely more than a few keystrokes embedded in an unrelated work file.

He's gone. They have him.

Ona inhaled slowly, forcing herself to remain still, to suppress the instinct to react. Think. Do not feel. Emotions were a liability now. Panic would only accelerate the collapse.

She knew what happened to workers who were taken for "reassignment." There were no trials, no hearings, no explanations. Once the system deemed you a threat, you ceased to exist in the way you had before. Your records were wiped, your assignments rewritten. The lucky ones were forced into the lower tiers of labor, reclassified into roles that guaranteed their obedience through exhaustion and deprivation. The unlucky ones simply vanished.

Joras would not survive in either scenario. And that meant she had no choice. She had to move.

Her mind raced through the possibilities, the calculations running parallel tracks. Escape was impossible. The complex was sealed, monitored at every level. But resistance was still an option. She still had access to the network. She still had information.

And more than that, she still had leverage.

Ona had spent years learning the intricacies of the system, mapping the ways in which power flowed through its invisible veins. The data she had gathered, the backdoor access points she had quietly logged, the security vulnerabilities that Capitalschism had dismissed as too minor to correct, these were her weapons now.

She sent a single message, encrypted, routed through a dozen false pathways.

Bring them to me. We end this tonight.

She would not let Joras be erased. She would not let the system win.

Joras did not know how long he had been confined. Time did not function properly in the holding cells. There were no clocks, no windows, nothing to mark the passing of hours or days. The walls were smooth, featureless, bathed in an artificial glow that never dimmed, never brightened. The only indication that he was still alive came in the form of the system's cold, methodical intrusions.

Routine sedation. Biometric scans. Neuromeric stability assessments. It was not torture in the traditional sense. There was no pain, no overt violence. Just the slow, deliberate unraveling of his identity. A recalibration.

Joras understood the process. It was designed to break him down, to rewrite him into something the system could use again. Opposition would be countered with isolation. Compliance would be rewarded with carefully controlled restoration.

He had seen it happen before. He had watched it in others. He would not let it happen to him.

The door to his cell slid open without warning. Two figures stepped inside. One was an officer, one of the nameless enforcers, his posture rigid, his expression unreadable. The other—

Joras inhaled sharply. It was someone he knew. A face from the movement. A face that had sat in their meetings, had spoken words of defiance, had promised loyalty. Betrayal had a name now.

The officer turned to the traitor. "We appreciate your cooperation."

Joras clenched his jaw. The system had found its crack. And now, it was going to use it.

Joras had always known that opposition carried a cost. He had accepted that risk when he first stepped beyond survival, when he first chose to see the system for what it was rather than simply enduring its weight. But betrayal, that was something else entirely.

He had spent weeks, months, trusting the people around him, believing that their suffering had bound them together in a way that the system could not touch. And yet, here he was, staring into the eyes of someone who had sat beside him in dimly lit corridors, whispering strategies for disruption, speaking of liberation as if it were possible. Now, that same face regarded him with a careful neutrality, a lack of expression that chilled him more than rage or regret ever could.

They weren't broken. They had chosen this.

The officer beside them was silent for a long moment, observing. Joras could feel the weight of the assessment, the methodical way the system processed human behavior, measuring responses, determining whether further pressure was necessary.

The enforcer finally spoke. "We don't want to waste valuable assets." His voice was calm, professional, completely detached. "Cooperation ensures continuity. Your knowledge is useful."

Joras did not respond.

The officer continued, as if reading from a script. "You have been classified as conditionally salvageable." He let the words settle before adding, "It would be unfortunate if you chose to render yourself otherwise."

Joras exhaled slowly, letting the silence stretch. He could feel the presence of the traitor beside the officer, their body language stiff, uncertain. There was no satisfaction in their expression, no arrogance. They had done what they thought necessary. He could see that now.

And that made it worse. Because it meant the system had not forced them into this choice. It had simply offered it. A bargain. A way out. And they had taken it.

The enforcer shifted slightly, as though adjusting his approach. "You may believe you have value to the opposition. But that is an illusion. The movement is compromised. We are already dismantling its structure." He gestured toward the traitor. "You are not the first to see reason."

Joras knew better than to take the bait. The system thrived on the illusion of inevitability, on convincing people that resistance was futile, that the machine was too large, too omnipresent, too absolute to challenge. He could not afford to let them see hesitation, doubt.

So he did what he had always done. He endured. He sat still, breathing evenly, ignoring the traitor beside him, ignoring the weight of the system pressing down on him.

Finally, the officer exhaled, a quiet acknowledgment of the impasse. "We'll speak again."

The door slid shut. Joras was alone again.

Ona moved quickly, methodically. There was no time for doubt.

She had known this moment would come, had always understood that their defiance could only remain invisible for so long. And so, while Joras had been the one moving within the opposition, she had been preparing. Watching. Learning. Mapping out possibilities. Now, with the system closing in, she had one thing left to do.

She had to buy them time.

The message she sent was short, encoded, buried within the system's logistics reports, a signal meant for only one set of eyes. Lian would understand.

Then, without hesitation, Ona erased her own data signature. For all intents and purposes, Ona no longer existed within the system. She had been studying its vulnerabilities for months, tracking the ways it monitored workers, the blind spots that Capitalschism had dismissed as too insignificant to patch. Those blind spots were her advantage now.

The moment Joras was taken, the system would begin recalibrating its assessment of her. They would be watching. They would expect panic, mistakes, desperate action. She would give them none of it.

Instead, she would disappear before they even realized what she was doing.

She had learned long ago that survival was about adaptation, not defiance. Resistance, when noticed too soon, was crushed before it could ever take form. The system did not punish rage, it erased it. It did not need to engage in open violence when it could simply rewrite a person's existence, reduce them to a statistic, an unaccounted inefficiency. Ona had watched it happen to others. She would not let it happen to Joras.

She kept moving, slipping through corridors, her body programmed to match the slow, automated rhythm of the complex. The system scanned movements for anomalies, for deviations from patterns of acceptable exhaustion. Workers who moved with intention were flagged. Workers who broke pace were tracked. But workers who looked tired, beaten down, resigned to their place? The system ignored them.

Ona counted on that now.

Joras did not know how much time had passed. Hours, maybe longer. The cell remained unchanged, the walls a featureless expanse of artificial sterility. But he had learned something valuable from that first encounter.

They weren't ready to break him. Not yet. That meant they were still unsure of how to proceed.

The system did not waste resources unless it had to. If they believed Joras was already beaten, they would have removed him immediately, assigned him to a lower-tier labor role, processed his existence into a routine function. The fact that they were still assessing him meant they had doubts. He could use that.

The door slid open again, and this time, he recognized the officer who entered. Callen. Joras tensed.
Callen had been a presence in their lives long before the resistance had begun. He had been Ona's direct overseer, the man who had dangled security in front of her like a leash, who

had ensured that every opportunity came at the cost of silent obedience. He had been watching them from the beginning.

Now, he smiled, a small, contained expression that did not reach his eyes.

"You've created quite the inconvenience," Callen said smoothly. He did not sit. Did not need to. His presence alone was an assertion of power.

Joras clenched his jaw, refusing to rise to the bait.

Callen studied him, as if he were something theoretical, something that needed to be quantified. "You're a logical man," he continued. "You understand the mathematics of survival. The odds of your movement's success. The risks of noncompliance."

He let the silence stretch before adding, "Ona does too."

Joras's fingers curled into fists.

Callen's smile widened slightly. "Do you think she'll make the same mistake you did?"

Joras inhaled slowly, forcing himself to remain still. He understood what Callen was doing. It was not a question. It was a seed, one meant to take root, to fester, to erode his certainty. He would not let it.

He lifted his chin, meeting Callen's gaze without flinching. "You don't understand her at all."

Callen tilted his head slightly, as if considering the statement, then stepped back. "We'll see."

And then, he left. Joras exhaled slowly. The system was moving faster now. But so was Ona.

Ona moved through the corridors of the complex as if nothing had changed. She kept her pace steady, her expression neutral, her body language calibrated to project exhaustion rather than urgency. Urgency was suspicious. Exhaustion was expected.

She had learned early that the system did not look for sudden, dramatic movements, it watched for deviations in routine. A worker who ran was a target. A worker who moved with too much purpose was a threat. But a worker who seemed beaten down, who carried themselves with the slow, mechanical efficiency of someone resigned to their place? That was someone the system ignored.

And so, she played the part.

Even as her mind raced, even as she calculated her next steps with precision, she let her posture sag, let the weight of her body sink into its movements. She avoided eye contact, made her way toward the supply sector with the same weary gait as the hundreds of others moving through their assigned pathways. She had two objectives.

The first was to erase her presence.

The digital signature she had scrubbed earlier would buy her some time, but it would not last forever. The system would eventually flag the discrepancy, detect the gap where her data should be, and begin looking for her. She had to ensure that when that moment came, there was nothing left for them to track.

The second was to reach Lian.

Lian had been running contingency plans for months, preparing for the moment when the system would shift from quiet suppression to open retaliation. Now, that moment had arrived. And if Ona was going to get Joras back, if they were going to survive this at all, they would need to act before Capitalschism fully locked them down.

She slipped into the supply corridor, making her way toward the terminal hub. A low-level technician sat behind the desk, barely glancing up as she approached. The system had long since trained its workers to ignore anything that did not explicitly require their attention. Ona took advantage of that fact now.

Her fingers moved quickly over the access panel, bypassing standard authentication, slipping through the cracks of the system's layered security. She had spent years learning how to move unseen within the machine. Now, she was using that knowledge to dismantle it.

A soft beep confirmed the update. She exhaled. Her file was gone. Not just erased, reassigned. To the system, she no longer existed as Ona. Her work profile had been shuffled, her records fragmented and rerouted through low-priority maintenance sectors, buried in algorithmic noise. When the system came looking, it would find nothing but dead ends. That would buy her at least a few hours.

She turned, stepping away from the terminal, just another exhausted worker leaving another monotonous task. Now, she had to find Lian. And after that, she had to get Joras out.

Joras sat in silence, his body still, his breathing measured.

He had been through every possible outcome in his mind, every scenario that could unfold from here. The system would not kill him. Not yet. He was still valuable to them, still a piece they could use, manipulate, extract from.

And as long as he was useful, he was still a variable they had not fully controlled.

That meant he had leverage. The door slid open again. Joras did not look up. A figure stepped inside, stopping just short of him. Then, after a long pause.

"She's still out there."
Joras exhaled slowly. He closed his eyes for just a moment.

Ona was still moving. And that meant there was still hope.

10
Rising TIDE

Joras had expected the movement to die after the crackdown. That was how it had always worked, resistance would rise, the system would retaliate, and the weight of consequences would crush whatever hope had ignited in the first place. That was how it had happened before. That was how the system had perfected its cycle of control.

But this time, something was different.

This time, people didn't retreat.

The moment Capitalschism executed its purge, workers who had never spoken to each other before began whispering in corridors. Those who had previously followed orders without question started hesitating, pausing just a little too long before confirming their tasks. Even those who had once believed compliance was survival began looking at their contracts with suspicion, asking the questions they had been too afraid to voice.

It was Lian who saw it first.

"They overplayed their hand," she said, standing in a dimly lit storeroom, speaking in the quiet, measured tone of someone who had just witnessed a fundamental shift in the system's balance. "They wanted to isolate us. Instead, they made us visible to each other."

Joras sat across from her, his body still aching from confinement, his mind still catching up to the fact that he was free, but not safe. Ona sat beside him, scanning through messages on a stolen device, tracking the movement of patrol units, mapping out the network of workers who were still willing to fight. The air around them buzzed with urgency, but also with something else, determination.

"They know our faces now," Joras said. "They won't let this happen again."

Lian exhaled. "Then we don't give them a single target."

And that was the beginning of TIDE (Target, Inspire, Disrupt, Empower).

The system thrived on predictability. That was its greatest weakness.

For decades, Capitalschism had perfected its model of control, refining its ability to suppress resistance before it could spread. It had designed algorithms that could identify dissent before it even fully formed, that could isolate individuals, apply pressure, reassign, reclassify, erase. It had conditioned workers to believe that rebellion was futile, that every act of defiance would only bring more suffering.

But TIDE didn't function like a traditional resistance.

It wasn't built on centralized leadership. It wasn't dependent on a single chain of command. It was everywhere and nowhere at once, a network of loosely connected cells, each capable of operating independently, each able to act even if the others fell.

It started small, messages passed through hidden subroutines, QR codes embedded in supply orders, signals buried in seemingly mundane scheduling updates. Workers who had once feared standing alone began forming alliances, structuring their movements around one simple truth:

The system could not function without them.

The first wave of defiance came in the form of small acts of disruption.

Delivery drivers who had once optimized their routes for speed began making unnecessary detours. Warehouse workers who had once completed their quotas with ruthless efficiency started making "accidental" inventory errors. Payment systems experienced mysterious lags, distribution schedules failed to meet their projected output.

At first, the system treated it as a statistical anomaly, an unexpected inefficiency that would be corrected through minor recalibrations. But as the disruptions spread, as the data models began to fail to predict the human element, it became clear that something larger was happening.

The workers weren't just slowing down. They were taking control.

The second wave was economic.

Capitalschism had always relied on a model of total dependency. Workers were paid, but the money flowed directly back into the system, rent, food, healthcare, transit, every necessity owned and regulated by the corporation. Wages were never truly earned. They were circulated.

TIDE broke that cycle.
They formed underground mutual aid networks, redistributing resources in ways the system could not track. Workers pooled their earnings, bypassing the automated deduction systems, purchasing supplies through external vendors, redistributing food in ways that bypassed corporate checkpoints.

They boycotted.

Not loudly. Not in ways that could be traced. But subtly, strategically. They stopped spending. Stopped engaging in the endless loop of consumption that Capitalschism had designed for them.

And for the first time in decades, the system felt the loss.

Joras had never imagined himself as a leader.

He had never seen himself as the kind of person who stood at the center of something larger than himself, who made speeches, who inspired others to action. But leadership wasn't about titles anymore. It wasn't about standing on a platform and rallying people to a cause.

It was about proving that survival was no longer enough.

Workers whispered his name in corridors. Not as a hero, not as a revolutionary, but as proof that defiance was possible. They had seen him taken. They had seen him return. And that was enough. Ona saw it happening before he did.

"You're becoming a symbol," she said one night, sitting beside him in the dim glow of an encrypted message screen. "Whether you want to be or not."

Joras exhaled. "I don't want to be."
She nodded. "But you are."
He had once believed that TIDE would rise without leaders. That it would spread without faces, that it would remain a decentralized force, too fluid to suppress. And in many ways, that was still true.

But symbols mattered. People needed something to hold onto. And somehow, he had become that. The realization settled into him like a weight, but not an unbearable one.

Because for the first time in his life, he wasn't just surviving. He was fighting for something more.

Joras had always thought of leadership as something external, something that happened to people who sought power, who thrived in the spotlight, who knew how to wield authority with precision and purpose. He had never seen himself as one of them.

But TIDE didn't have leaders in the traditional sense.

It wasn't structured like a corporation, or even like the old labor unions from a past so thoroughly dismantled that most workers only knew of them through restricted archives. TIDE was a force, not an organization. It moved through networks rather than hierarchies, adapting as quickly as the system tried to contain it.

And yet, somehow, his name had become attached to it.

It had started in whispers. Joras is back. It had spread through encrypted channels. They took him, and he survived. It had woven itself into the very fabric of their quiet rebellion. If he can keep going, so can we.

Joras didn't know what it meant to be a leader when there was no official movement, no centralized structure to guide. But as the resistance deepened, as Capitalschism began struggling to contain something it did not fully understand, he realized that leadership wasn't about control. It was about being seen.

And he was being seen.

The moment he stepped back onto the warehouse floor, the moment his presence was confirmed by those who had assumed he was already gone, everything changed.

The boycotts were working.

Not in an obvious, dramatic way, but in the slow, grinding way that systems failed, not through collapse, but through corrosion.

The first signs were algorithmic inconsistencies. Supply chains lagged. Inventory miscalculations increased. Automated cost projections failed to predict fluctuations that should have been impossible under the system's strict regulatory models.

It was happening because workers were making choices that were not being recorded.

For years, Capitalschism had perfected the illusion of free markets, a system where workers were paid, but only in ways that ensured their wages returned to the same machine that had issued them. It had been designed to be inescapable.

But TIDE had found a way around it.

It had started small.

A group of warehouse workers began rerouting excess food shipments. Not large enough to be flagged as theft, but enough to disrupt the company's profit margins in imperceptible ways. Workers in logistics sectors began manipulating system logs, adding subtle inefficiencies that forced automated processes into an endless loop of recalibration.

And then came the real attack.

Capitalschism's payment systems had always been linked to its internal financial networks. Workers were paid through company-issued accounts, their wages automatically allocated to predetermined expenses, housing, food, healthcare, debt repayment.

TIDE severed the loop.

Through a coordinated effort of programmers, logistics teams, and workers who had spent years navigating the system's labyrinthine contracts, they disconnected thousands of employees from company-controlled payment structures.

The result was immediate and catastrophic.

Workers suddenly had access to money that Capitalschism could not track. Instead of wages being automatically extracted through pre-approved corporate expenditures, workers began moving their funds outside the system.

The corporation panicked.

Automated rent deductions failed. Meal allocations became inconsistent. Predictive economic models collapsed under the weight of human unpredictability. And for the first time in its existence, Capitalschism felt something close to fear.

Joras did not plan the next phase of opposition. It happened without his input, without his control, without anyone dictating orders. It spread because it was inevitable.
Workers in separate divisions, people who had never met, never spoken, who had never seen themselves as part of a greater whole, began acting with shared purpose.

The factory sectors reduced their output in ways the system could not trace. The transportation hubs deliberately slowed shipments. Even the security forces, those who had once enforced compliance without question, began to falter.

Because now, even they were starting to understand something crucial. The machine had no power of its own. It only functioned because people let it.

And now? Now, the people were deciding otherwise.

Joras sat in the shadows of a converted storage bay, listening as messages flowed through encrypted relays. Lian was with him, her fingers moving over a handheld console, watching as data packets bounced through a decentralized web of communication points.

"We're in over twenty sectors now," she murmured, scanning the latest reports. "It's spreading beyond us."

Joras exhaled, pressing his hands against his knees. He was exhausted, his body still recovering from the confinement he had endured, but his mind was clear.

"They're adapting," he said. "So will the system."

Lian nodded. "Capitalschism won't let this last. They'll shift strategies soon."

Joras knew that. He had spent too much time inside the machine not to know how it would respond. The corporation had built its empire on the assumption that human behavior could be controlled, predicted, managed. It had never accounted for human choice. And that was what TIDE had become. Not a revolution. Not a rebellion. A choice. A choice to say no. A choice to make the machine work for them, or to let it fail.

Ona sat nearby, silent, watching the messages unfold. She had always been the strategist, the one who saw the vulnerabilities before anyone else.

"They're going to try to cut us off," she said finally. "If they can't contain us internally, they'll isolate us from the outside world."

Joras nodded. "Then we get ahead of them."

Lian glanced up. "How?"

Joras exhaled. "We bring in more."

The others stared at him.

"The system only survives because people believe there's no alternative," he continued. "But now? We are the alternative. And if we can convince them that they have a choice…"

He trailed off, but Ona understood immediately. Lian did too. TIDE wasn't just about defying Capitalschism. It wasn't about sabotage or disruption or economic resistance. It was about proving that another world was possible. For years, workers had accepted the system because they had been told there was nothing else.

TIDE was proving them wrong.

And if they could convince more people of that truth, Capitalschism wouldn't be able to stop them. Because the machine could not function if no one agreed to run it.
Joras closed his eyes for just a moment, letting the realization settle. They weren't just fighting anymore. They were building something new.

Joras had never seen a machine collapse before. He had read about it, had studied the histories that the system had tried to erase, how great empires fell not in a single moment, not through war or rebellion, but through something quieter, something slower. Withdrawing consent. Refusing to comply. Choosing to step away from the wheel and let it spin itself into destruction.

TIDE was no longer a whisper. It was no longer a few workers passing messages in dark corridors, no longer a handful of disruptors nudging the system into inefficiency. It had become an inevitability. The machine could not function without its gears, and now, those gears had begun to break away.

The response from Capitalschism was swift. First, they increased wages in select sectors, attempting to buy loyalty from those who might still hesitate. Then, when that failed to slow the spread of resistance, they offered promotions, artificial advancement into slightly less brutal conditions, designed to keep people invested in the system, to make them believe escape was unnecessary when they could simply climb the ranks instead.

But no one believed them anymore.

The facade had cracked. People saw the system for what it was, not as a source of security, but as a cage. The higher wages came with new deductions. The promotions came with longer contracts, deeper dependencies, more insidious forms of control. Workers who had once feared questioning their place now saw the truth: there was no safety in obedience.

And so, they stopped playing the game.

They left their shifts early in coordinated waves, walking out without warning, forcing supply chains to fall apart in real-time. They refused automated scheduling updates, letting their work assignments lapse into unfilled voids, grinding the algorithm to a halt. In some divisions, workers showed up, but did nothing, standing silently at their stations, letting production plummet as the system failed to calculate the missing output.

And then the outside world noticed.

TIDE had been careful to grow in the shadows, to remain invisible to the media channels still controlled by corporate hands. But now, it was everywhere. Leaks from internal networks had reached independent journalists, encrypted feeds showing the breakdown of Capitalschism's once-infallible efficiency. The narrative was shifting.

The corporation did not control the story anymore. And that was the moment it truly began to panic.

Joras had never thought of himself as a revolutionary. Even now, as he stood in the middle of a quiet, darkened assembly hall, once a mandatory training center for efficiency compliance, now repurposed as a gathering point for workers preparing their next coordinated action, he could feel the weight of expectation pressing against him. They looked to him not as a commander, not as an organizer, but as a symbol. And symbols could not afford to break.

Ona stood beside him, watching as more workers arrived. She had always been the one who saw the fractures before they widened, the one who could map the next stage of resistance before the system even realized what was happening. Now, as she glanced at Joras, he could see something in her expression that had not been there before. Conviction. The fear was still there, it would never fully leave them. But now, something else had taken root alongside it. Hope. And hope was dangerous. Hope spread like an untended fire, igniting where the system had long believed only submission could exist. Hope was the one variable the system had never accounted for.

Lian stepped forward. "It's happening faster than we expected."

Joras nodded. "We need to be ready for the next move."

Capitalschism would not let this stand. That was the certainty they all understood.

The corporation had spent decades perfecting its control, refining its methods of suppression, ensuring that no uprising could ever reach the point of momentum. But TIDE had already passed that point. They weren't just disrupting the system. They were building something new in its place.

"We need to secure the networks," Ona said, pulling up a projection of system vulnerabilities. "They'll try to isolate us. If they can't control the workers, they'll control communication. We need to make sure we stay connected."

Joras exhaled. "And when that fails?"

Lian smirked. "Then we do what we've already been doing."

She let the words settle before adding, "We keep going. And we don't stop."

Joras looked around the room, at the faces of those who had once been strangers to him. They weren't strangers anymore. They were allies. They were fighters. They were a movement.

And the machine? It was already failing.

Not all at once, not in a dramatic collapse, but in a slow, grinding way, the same way it had taken power in the first place. Bit by bit. Piece by piece. Not with one great strike, but with a thousand quiet refusals, a thousand small acts of defiance that would add up to something unstoppable.

They had always believed that the system was too large to fight. Now, they were proving it was too fragile to survive. The walls of control were not indestructible. They were made of contracts, numbers, automated decisions, and invisible rules, and all of them could be rewritten, disrupted, dismantled.

Joras had once believed that survival was the only goal. Now, survival wasn't enough. They weren't just resisting anymore. They were taking back their future.

11
The Jungle Burns

Joras hadn't expected victory to feel so precarious. He had spent so long imagining the collapse of Capitalschism as something definitive, a moment of rupture, a breaking point where the system would simply cease to function. But revolutions were never that simple.

When the first leaks hit the networks, they spread faster than anyone had anticipated. Encrypted data packets surfaced across underground channels, revealing internal reports, financial manipulations, records of worker deaths hidden under efficiency protocols, the full extent of how deeply Capitalschism had embedded itself in the governing structures of the city. It wasn't just a corporation. It was the system itself.

TIDE had prepared for retaliation, but they hadn't expected the truth to move this quickly. It wasn't just workers who saw it now. It was consumers, investors, city officials, people who had long benefited from the machine but had never truly seen its gears turning. And for the first time, the machine hesitated.

Joras sat in the dim light of a repurposed storage unit, watching as messages flooded across the network. Lian was pacing, her fingers moving rapidly over a device, tracking responses in real-time. Ona sat beside him, scanning through reactions from media outlets, some trying to bury the leaks, others struggling to spin them into justifications.

"The stock just dropped ten percent," Lian murmured, more to herself than anyone else. "They're bleeding."
Joras exhaled. It wasn't enough to kill them. Not yet. But it was a wound.

"This isn't the end," Ona said, her voice calm but firm. "This is the moment they dig in."

She was right. Capitalschism had spent decades preparing for something like this. They had built their power on the assumption that control could always be reasserted, that the system could always course-correct, that people would panic but ultimately fall back in line. And so, they did what every empire did when faced with collapse. They tightened their grip.

The first response came from the board of directors, a carefully crafted statement of denial. The leaks were misinterpreted. The records had been taken out of context. The financial discrepancies were necessary adjustments to ensure economic stability. The deaths? Statistical anomalies. The corporate media outlets amplified the message, shifting focus onto TIDE itself. Who were these people? Were they terrorists? Criminals? Agents of chaos?

The newscasts displayed doctored images of supposed "ringleaders," spliced together from public surveillance feeds, making resistance seem like an act of personal ambition rather than a collective movement. Joras's name surfaced, his image appearing alongside headlines that framed him as a dangerous agitator.

Ona scrolled through the coverage, her expression unreadable. "They're trying to make you the villain."

Joras let out a bitter chuckle. "I was never the hero."

Lian shook her head. "They're making a mistake."
"They think they can cut off the movement by taking out the figurehead," Ona said. "But we were never built like that."

TIDE wasn't a single leader. It wasn't an organization with a chain of command. It was an ecosystem, one that had learned to evolve faster than the machine that sought to control it. And Capitalschism had miscalculated.

The city's political structure had always been an extension of corporate interests, but now the pressure was mounting from all sides. Consumers were canceling subscriptions to Capitalschism-owned services. Investors were pulling back, watching the instability spread. Workers who had never considered joining TIDE were suddenly paying attention. And so, the corporation did what it had always done. It turned to the politicians it had purchased.

Within hours, lawmakers issued emergency resolutions, condemning "anti-corporate extremism" as a direct threat to economic security. New bills were introduced, legislation designed to suppress worker-led boycotts, crack down on decentralized organizing, classify disruption of automated labor systems as acts of "economic sabotage."

"This is where they fight back," Lian muttered. "They know they can't stop us from the inside, so they'll try to criminalize us from the outside."

Joras felt the weight of the moment settle over him. They had seen this playbook before. Every movement that had ever threatened power had met this same response. The opposition would be rebranded as criminals, radicals, anarchists. The public would be told that, yes, the system needed reform, but not like this. Not through disorder. Not through rebellion. And slowly, the pressure to return to "normal" would begin.

Ona locked eyes with him. "We have to make a choice."

Joras nodded. "Do we escalate?"

Lian exhaled. "If we do, we have to be ready for what comes next."

Because this was the threshold. They had wounded the beast, but the beast had more power than any one of them could comprehend.

The board of directors convened in secret, but secrets didn't last long anymore. TIDE had infiltrated enough of the system to track their decisions in real time. Capitalschism was preparing to make a final move. The executives had reached out to higher authorities, military contractors, intelligence firms, security specialists. The corporation had always functioned as its own government, but now, it was beginning to act like one.

"They're preparing for a full-scale crackdown," Ona murmured, reading through intercepted transmissions. "They'll frame it as a necessary step to restore order."

Joras exhaled slowly. This was always going to happen. For months, they had fought in the shadows, using the system's own rules against it, leveraging its inefficiencies, exploiting its blind spots. But now, the machine was shifting tactics. It would not be gradual anymore. It would not be quiet.

It would burn everything.

Joras stood at the edge of the district, looking out over the skyline of the city that had never truly belonged to the people who kept it running. This was not victory. Not yet. The revolution was still unfinished, uncertain, fragile. But for the first time, Capitalschism was afraid. And that meant something. The machine was no longer invincible. The cracks had become fractures, the fractures had become fault lines, and sooner or later, something would break.

Ona came to stand beside him. "What do we do now?"

Joras clenched his jaw. "We don't let them decide what happens next."

Because the jungle was already burning. And TIDE wasn't going to stop the fire. They were going to spread it.

The system was shifting into its final defense. Joras could feel it in the air, in the way the media's tone had sharpened overnight, in the way the security presence around key infrastructure had subtly increased. Capitalschism was preparing to move. Not through quiet recalibrations or algorithmic adjustments, not through the incremental suffocation of dissent that had worked so well for so long. This time, it would be open.

For decades, the corporation had relied on a strategy of containment. It had engineered an economic system that rendered resistance futile, creating a prison without walls, where workers were too dependent to revolt. If someone fought back, they were absorbed, reassigned, their discontent redirected into the endless churn of productivity.

But TIDE had proven something Capitalschism had not prepared for. Once people saw the machine, really saw it, saw the mechanisms that kept them trapped, saw the empty promises of advancement, saw that their suffering was not a personal failure but a deliberate function of the system itself, they could no longer be contained. And so, the corporation turned to its oldest weapon. Fear.

The crackdown began as a whisper, a trickle of new regulations, a subtle shift in enforcement. A few workers arrested under obscure infractions, their names scrubbed from records, their work permits revoked. Warnings sent to the more cautious defectors, the ones who had not yet fully committed to TIDE but had shown signs of hesitation in their compliance. Then, the laws were passed.

Legislation introduced overnight. Sweeping, ambiguous statutes meant to outlaw not just dissent, but even the mere possibility of organizing. The language was familiar: "National security." "Economic stability." "Preventing disruption."

A digital strike? Economic terrorism. Withholding labor? Criminal collusion. Information leaks? High-tech sedition. The boardroom strategies were simple, make resistance illegal. Make the cost unbearable. Force people to choose between survival and revolution.

Joras watched the announcements play out on the giant public feeds, official statements from corporate-aligned politicians, handpicked analysts explaining why worker uprisings destabilized economic confidence, why protecting efficiency was paramount. And, of course, his name.

His image, displayed in stark contrast on every news cycle. Not as a worker, not as a survivor, not as someone who had only ever fought for the right to live without being bled dry. No, he had been rebranded as something else entirely. A radical. A terrorist. A traitor to progress.

Ona switched off the display, her expression unreadable.

“They want a face for this,” she said. “They want a villain.”

Joras exhaled, running a hand over his face. “It won’t work.”

Lian leaned against the wall. “It doesn’t need to work. It just needs to be loud enough to make people hesitate.”

That was the real battle now. Not the laws, not the security reinforcements, not the arrests. Hesitation. Doubt. Capitalschism had spent years engineering a world where fear dictated every decision. Where taking risks was a death sentence, where stability, no matter how brutal, was always the safer choice. Now, all they had to do was remind people of that. Make them doubt. Make them second-guess. Make them afraid that standing up meant losing everything.

“They’re calling for an emergency summit with the city’s leadership,” Ona said, scanning the encrypted reports. “Capitalschism wants new enforcement measures approved by morning.”

Joras set his jaw. That meant they were panicking. They wouldn’t be making these moves if they still believed they could contain this.

“Then we have to move faster,” Lian said.

Joras nodded. They had expected escalation. Now, they had to meet it.

The second wave of suppression was not subtle. Within twenty-four hours, armored security units were deployed around Capitalschism-controlled housing complexes. Not for protection. For control. Checkpoints appeared overnight, scanning workers as they moved through the districts, tagging individuals with behavioral compliance scores A new metric, unknown to workers until now. Joras heard the reports filtering in from the underground networks.

"People are being flagged."
"They're reassigning defectors without warning."

"They're targeting anyone linked to us."

That was how the system adapted. Not by acknowledging the resistance, not by engaging in open battle, but by twisting its reach into something so total, so absolute, that people felt their choices disappear before they even made them. And yet, the fear wasn't working the way it used to. Not entirely.

Yes, some people hesitated. Yes, some turned away from TIDE, resigned to survival. But others, more than Joras had expected, stood firm. And it wasn't just the factory workers now. It was engineers. Programmers. Low-level managers. Logistics coordinators. People who had once believed they were separate from the exploited masses, who had held onto the illusion of security until now.

But Capitalschism had revealed its hand too soon. And now, they saw it. TIDE had begun in shadows. In whispers. In slow, cautious steps. But now? Now it was wildfire.

Joras stood before a crowd of workers in a repurposed industrial warehouse, his voice steady despite the weight of the moment.

"This is the choice they're forcing," he said, looking out at the faces around him. "They want us to believe we only have two options, compliance or destruction."

Silence. No one moved. No one breathed.

"But they're wrong," he continued. "Because there is a third option."

He let the words settle, let the weight of them press into the room, into the bones of the people who had been waiting for someone to name what they already knew.

"We build something else."

A murmur rippled through the gathering. Not resistance. Recognition. Because that was the truth none of them had been willing to say out loud. TIDE had started as disruption. It had started as an opposition, as a way to break the machine, to slow it down, to fight against the tide of exploitation.

But that wasn't enough anymore. They couldn't just dismantle the system. They had to replace it. And for the first time, the workers around him didn't just look afraid. They looked ready.

Joras exhaled, his hands clenched at his sides. The jungle was already burning. And now it was time to decide what would grow from the ashes.

12
The New Dawn

Joras had never imagined a future beyond survival. His life, for as long as he could remember, had been dictated by scarcity, of time, of choices, of the illusion that anything could ever truly belong to him. But now, for the first time, the horizon stretched beyond the machine.

They had not won. Not yet. Capitalschism still existed, wounded, reeling, adapting to the cracks in its foundation, but it was not yet broken. The system did not fall in a single moment. It eroded, piece by piece, collapsing under the weight of its own excess, its own inability to bend without eventually snapping. TIDE had not just been an opposition movement. It had become something more.

A beginning.

The settlement had no name. It was a patchwork of repurposed industrial buildings, reclaimed from abandoned supply hubs and forgotten manufacturing plants, places once optimized for maximum corporate extraction, now transformed into something entirely new. A community. Not a city, not yet. But something close. The first few weeks had been chaos, finding shelter, securing food, establishing a new infrastructure independent of the corporate economy. The old system was still trying to smother them, still attempting to starve them out, still sending operatives to disrupt, infiltrate, reassert control. But the machine was no longer omnipotent. People had begun choosing not to comply. That was the real revolution.

Not the dramatic battles, not the moments of resistance that had captured headlines, but the quiet refusal, the rejection of dependency, the simple act of stepping away. For years, they had been told the system was inescapable. That the world outside corporate governance was chaos, that without economic oversight, civilization itself would collapse. Now, they were proving otherwise.

Joras walked through the settlement, his steps slow, deliberate. It still felt fragile. Every structure, every system they had built, from communal food distribution to encrypted trade networks to the independent energy grids they were slowly assembling, all of it existed on the edge of collapse. But it existed. That alone was enough.

Ona was speaking with a group of organizers near one of the central hubs, her posture relaxed in a way Joras had rarely seen before. She had always been the one to see beyond survival, beyond the immediate struggle, beyond the next desperate step.

Now, she was building something permanent.

He approached as the conversation shifted, the topic moving from resource allocation to long-term infrastructure.

"We need redundancy," Ona was saying. "Capitalschism won't let this stand. They're going to try to make an example of us, whether that means economic retaliation or direct force. If we want this to last, we can't just build it. We have to make sure it can't be erased."

Lian nodded, adjusting the interface on her wrist. "The encryption networks are stable for now, but we need more than that. If they shut down our access points, we're back in the dark."

A coder named Arun spoke up. "We need to create something they can't shut down. A system that isn't just decentralized, but entirely independent."

Joras frowned. "You mean… outside the internet?"

"Outside their internet," Arun corrected. "The infrastructure is already in place. We don't need to build from scratch, we just need to redirect it. A new framework, built by us, controlled by no one."

Ona exhaled. "And from there?"

Arun met her gaze.

"From there, we replace everything."

The idea spread faster than anything they had built before. TIDE had spent years dismantling the machine from the inside, weakening its grip, exposing its vulnerabilities. Now, they were going to make it irrelevant.

The core of the new system was simple, a governance model that could not be bought, could not be manipulated, could not be controlled by those with wealth and power. Not a government. Not a corporation. Something new. A collective intelligence. Decisions would not be made in secret, hidden behind closed doors, dictated by boardrooms or technocrats or billionaire-backed politicians. They would be made openly, in real time, by the people who actually lived under them.

A system where voting wasn't an event, but a process. Where policies were not dictated from above, but shaped by those who would feel their consequences.

A society run by information, not capital.

And the key?

The Pinkprint.

The Pinkprint had been erased from every official archive. It had been banned outright, labeled dangerous, subversive, a threat to national stability. It had been buried. But information never truly disappeared.

The once-outlawed alternative to Project 2025, the blueprint for a system rooted not in greed, not in extraction, not in the hoarding of resources by an elite ruling class, but in something else entirely.

Empathy. Compassion. Fairness.

It was not a manifesto. It was a framework. A set of policies that valued collective well-being over corporate expansion, that prioritized sustainability over infinite growth, that placed power in the hands of the many rather than the few.

Worker-owned cooperatives.

A universal economy built not on competition, but collaboration.

A system where billionaires, where even multi-millionaires, could not exist, because wealth was no longer a tool of dominance or a value system, but a resource meant to be shared.

Infrastructure, energy, transportation, healthcare, even AI, not controlled by private interests, but by the communities who relied on them.

Joras listened as the coders debated implementation, as the organizers mapped out strategy, as the vision of something larger, something beyond resistance, beyond survival, beyond even TIDE itself, began to take shape.

And for the first time, he believed.

The system had always framed rebellion as a moment, a singular event, an outburst of chaos that would eventually be contained. But this was not a moment. This was a beginning. TIDE had always been more than a movement. It was an inevitability. The machine was failing, and they would not rebuild it. They would build something else. Joras met Ona's gaze. She already knew.

"Are we ready for this?" he asked.

Ona exhaled. "We don't have to be ready."

She glanced at the growing settlement around them. At the people who had chosen to walk away from the machine, the ones who had learned to govern themselves, the ones who had stopped waiting for permission to build something better.

"We just have to start."

Joras looked out at the horizon, a world not yet shaped, a system not yet written. The future felt like theirs. He had always thought the end of the system would be violent. And imagined the downfall of Capitalschism as something cinematic, a singular moment of collapse, a sudden and unmistakable rupture where the machine ground to a halt, sparks flying, its gears stripped and broken beyond repair. He had thought that change would come all at once, that revolution would be an event, not a process. But he had been wrong. Revolutions did not happen in a moment. They happened in a thousand choices, a thousand small refusals, a thousand acts of defiance that coalesced into something unstoppable. And now, he was watching it unfold, not as destruction, but as creation.

The infrastructure of the settlement was growing faster than even the most optimistic projections had anticipated. At first, it had been a handful of makeshift shelters, reclaimed buildings turned into communal living spaces, independent energy grids hacked together from salvaged technology. But now, it was something more. The core of their survival had been redundancy. No single failure point. No leader whose downfall would mean collapse. No single source of power that could be bought, threatened, or manipulated.

The people who had fled here had built everything themselves. Self-sustaining food systems, decentralized currency networks, alternative energy sources. They had learned from history. They had learned from the mistakes of revolutions past, from the cautionary tales of movements that had sought to dismantle power only to replace it with another version of the same thing. This time, there would be no singular seat of control. This time, power would belong to the many.

Ona stood at the center of one of the main hubs, scanning through a series of logistical updates. The settlement was still fragile, but it was holding. Every system they built had been designed with one fundamental principle, it could not be taken away. The food was not distributed by corporations but by the people who grew it. The water was not controlled by private entities but by the communities who maintained it. The communication networks were not dependent on centralized providers but run through a mesh of encrypted nodes, impossible to sever. Everything belonged to the people who used it. And that meant it could not be bought back into the machine. Joras approached as Ona finished her latest report, her fingers moving swiftly over her tablet.

"They're testing the perimeter again," she said without looking up.

Joras exhaled. "They won't stop."

Capitalschism had not given up. Not yet.

They had lost control of this settlement, but they were recalibrating, watching, waiting. The corporation did not fight battles it wasn't sure it could win. It was waiting for them to fail, waiting for cracks to form, waiting for the moment when exhaustion and uncertainty would weaken their resolve. But that moment was not coming. Joras looked around at the growing community, at the people working together, not out of obligation, not out of fear, but because they had chosen to.

"Let them wait," he muttered. "We're not going anywhere."

The new world they were building was unlike anything that had existed before. Not because the ideas were new, they weren't. Worker-owned industries, universal access to resources, direct democracy, these had all been proposed before, fought for before, even partially realized before. But every attempt had been undermined by the same thing:

The people in power had never let it last. Every time a cooperative movement had gained momentum, it had been crushed. By corporations. By governments. By billionaires who refused to tolerate a system where wealth was not hoarded but shared. This time, they would not be stopped. Not because they had greater numbers or better weapons or more resources, but because the system itself was failing, and nothing could save it now.

Capitalschism had always operated on the assumption that people would never fully walk away. That they would resist, yes, but ultimately they would negotiate, they would concede, they would agree to a reformed version of the same broken system.

But now, the system had nothing left to offer them.

They had already built something better.

The framework for the next stage of TIDE was nearly complete. Arun had been leading the digital infrastructure effort, mapping out the final layers of their new governance model.

"We don't need representation," he said, tapping the schematic on his screen. "We need participation."

Joras frowned. "How do you get that at scale?"

Arun looked up. "We do what they never wanted us to do. We put democracy in everyone's hands."

Not voting once every few years. Not delegating power to politicians who could be corrupted, bought, influenced. A governance system where every decision, every policy, every budget allocation, every law, was decided in real time, by the people who actually lived under it. The device in Arun's hand was unremarkable. A standard-issue interface, the kind used in every corporate city across the world. But what was inside it was something entirely new.

Joras studied the interface. "How does it work?"

"It's simple," Arun said. "Every person gets a direct say. No intermediaries. No bureaucrats. No politicians. Just real-time votes, real-time transparency, real-time policy creation."

Joras let out a low breath. "And it's unhackable?"

Arun smirked. "Nothing's unhackable. But it's decentralized. There's no server to take down, no single point of failure. It runs on peer-to-peer encryption, distributed across thousands of independent nodes. Even if they shut down half the network, the rest stays online."

Ona leaned forward. "And if they try to outlaw it?"

Arun's expression darkened. "Then we know we've already won."

Because if true democracy was illegal, then the system had already exposed itself. And once people saw that, there was no going back.

Joras stepped outside, watching the sun dip below the skyline. The remnants of the old world still loomed in the distance,

Capitalschism's towers, the endless corridors of power that had once seemed unshakable. But they were shaking now. The machine was still running, still trying to reclaim control, still holding onto whatever pieces of dominance it could. But its foundation was crumbling. TIDE had once been about breaking the machine. Now, it was about making sure nothing like it could ever rise again.

They would not negotiate with billionaires.

They would not allow a new elite to take power.

They would not let corporations dictate human life.

This was not reform.

This was replacement.

The Pinkprint was more than just an idea now. It was a plan, a system, a world in the making. A society where power belonged not to the wealthy, not to politicians, not to executives, but to the people.

No billionaires. No multi-millionaires. No corporate overlords.

Just a world where resources were shared, where decisions were made collectively, where no one was disposable.

Joras clenched his fists.

The old world had already burned.

Now, it was time to build the new one.

The old world was still standing. Barely. From a distance, Capitalschism's towers still gleamed, their glass exteriors reflecting the setting sun like monuments to a world that refused to acknowledge its own decay. The stock markets still flickered, recalibrating losses, redistributing wealth among the same power brokers who had orchestrated every crisis before. The media still broadcasted their narratives, spinning the collapse of the corporate state as a temporary disruption, a solvable anomaly, a momentary lapse in governance that would soon be corrected. But this time, there would be no correction.

Joras stood on the outskirts of the settlement, watching as the infrastructure of a new world took root in the ruins of the old.

This was not a city. Not in the way the system had defined cities. There were no corporate-owned developments, no walled enclaves where the wealthy hoarded comfort while the workers burned through their bodies for the illusion of survival.

This was something else. A self-sustaining network.

A place where housing was not a privilege but a necessity, where food was not a commodity but a shared resource, where decisions were not dictated by an invisible elite but made collectively, transparently, in real time.

It had taken months to reach this point, but they had done it.

And now, it was time for the next phase.

Ona approached, a tablet in hand, her expression unreadable.

"They know," she said simply.

Joras exhaled. "Of course they do."

Capitalschism had been watching, waiting for a moment of weakness. Their surveillance networks had not been entirely dismantled, just decentralized, disrupted, forced into obsolescence piece by piece. But the corporation still had eyes. Still had data streams. Still had the power to influence.

"They're trying to frame this as a separatist movement," Ona continued. "A rogue state. Something dangerous."

Joras smirked bitterly. "Of course they are."

The system had never feared resistance. It had accounted for that. The real threat was proof that people could live without it. Capitalschism could not afford for this to succeed. Not because of what was happening here, but because of what would come next. If this model worked, if TIDE proved that workers did not need corporations, that governance did not require billionaires, that economies did not have to function as systems of control, then the illusion would shatter. And when the illusion shattered, the empire would collapse.

Ona passed him the tablet. "They've started freezing accounts. Cutting off access to digital infrastructure. We knew this was coming."

Joras studied the reports. Power struggles were nothing new. Every revolution had reached this moment, the point where the old system, unable to win the battle outright, resorted to economic siege. But they had been preparing for this.

"Then we move faster," Joras said. "We implement it now."

Ona nodded. She had been waiting for this decision.

The coders had been working in shifts, building a governance system that could not be corrupted, that could not be manipulated, that could not be bought. A system that would replace capitalism entirely.

They had mapped it out. Modeled it. Stress-tested it. The framework had been built over the past decade by underground developers, people who had long known that the battle for power would not be fought in boardrooms or on factory floors, but in the architecture of information itself.

The final version was ready.

Joras stood in the central hub as Arun, Lian, and the other developers gathered around the network servers. This was the moment everything changed.

"We roll it out in stages," Arun said, fingers moving rapidly across his interface. "The first layer integrates into the existing infrastructure, encrypted digital identity, decentralized access points, secure voting modules. No more intermediaries, no more bureaucrats, no more politicians."

Lian nodded. "Stage two replaces financial transactions. Worker-owned banking networks, universal credit systems, economic decentralization. No billionaires. No corporate wealth hoarding. Every credit stays within the community."

"And then?" Joras asked.

Arun exhaled, looking up. "Then we implement The Pinkprint."

The Pinkprint had started as a theory, an alternative to the corporate governance of Project 2025, banned, buried, erased from the public consciousness. But information had a way of surviving. Now, it was here. A new model of governance. A system built on collective decision-making, where policies were not dictated from above but formed in real time through direct participation. It was not a government. It was a network. Every citizen would have access. Every vote, every policy, every decision, transparent, secure, immediate. There would be no representatives. No rulers. No gatekeepers. For the first time, people would govern themselves.

Joras looked at the data streams lighting up across the network. They were already integrating.

"This is it," Ona murmured. "This is what comes next."

Joras exhaled, the weight of the moment settling over him. They had spent so long fighting to tear the machine apart. Now, they were building something in its place. And Capitalschism? It could not adapt to this. This was a system beyond its reach.

The city was changing. The corporate strongholds still stood, but their foundations were rotting. The centralized banks were still issuing transactions, but fewer and fewer people were using them. The machine was still running, but it was running on empty. And the settlements? They were growing. The old world had lost its leverage. Billionaires could no longer manipulate a system that no longer required them. Corporations could not enforce their will when their economy had been abandoned.

Joras looked around at the people, the workers, the engineers, the families who had once been trapped in the endless cycle of debt and exploitation. They were free now. Not because the system had collapsed, but because they had walked away. TIDE had not just won. TIDE had made the old world irrelevant.

And now, they would make sure it never returned.

The final phase was already in motion. The Pinkprint's policies were being codified, not through laws, not through governing bodies, but through a self-regulating framework that required no authority. Worker-owned cooperatives were expanding.

Utilities, including the internet, including AI, were being transferred into collective ownership, no longer serving the interests of a few but belonging to the many. The concept of wealth itself was shifting. Not toward accumulation, but toward sustainability. Capitalschism had spent decades programming people to believe that their survival depended on the system. Now, the system depended on them. And they had chosen to let it die.

Joras turned toward Ona, the sky darkening behind them, the glow of the settlement spreading across the landscape like a new kind of sunrise.

Ona met his gaze.

"We did it," she said.

Joras nodded. “And now we keep going.”

Because this was not the end.

This was the beginning of something bigger than any of them had ever imagined.

About EATMS Productions

What's happening to women now is not random. It's structural.

Policy, culture, technology, and power are moving in the same direction.

EATMS maps them clearly and shows how to respond.

This title is part of an ongoing body of work. All EATMS Productions titles, across all series, authors, and formats, are components of a single connected project.

Start here: EATMS System Primer — Free Bundle
https://eatms.gumroad.com/l/dyvzbw

For full catalog or inquiries: eatms.me

Free survival booklet + EATMS updates: email "EATMS" to eatms@pm.me

Please feel free to burn part or all of this book, safely, as an effigy.

www.ingramcontent.com/pod-product-compliance
Lightning Source LLC
LaVergne TN
LVHW051001080826
845145LV00009B/2392

* 9 7 8 1 9 6 6 0 1 4 1 8 8 *